Shelf Life

Robert Corbet
AR B.L.: 4.9
Points: 5.0   UG

SHELF LIFE

ROBERT CORBET

Walker & Company
New York

First published in 2004 as *Shelf Life* in Australia by Allen & Unwin. First published in the United States of America in 2005 by Walker Publishing Company, Inc.

Published simultaneously in Canada by Fitzhenry and Whiteside, Markham, Ontario L3R 4T8

For information about permission to reproduce selections from this book, write to Permissions, Walker & Company, 104 Fifth Avenue, New York, New York 10011

Library of Congress Cataloging-in-Publication Data

Corbet, Robert, 1959–
  Shelf life / Robert Corbet.
      p.   cm.
  Summary: An assortment of teens working in a supermarket cope with health and family problems, future hopes and dreams, the complications of on-the-job romances, and the challenges of customer service.
  ISBN 0-8027-8959-5
  [1. Supermarkets—Fiction.   2. Interpersonal relations—Fiction.]
I. Title.

PZ7.C7983Sh 2005
[Fic]—dc22

                                                          2004058059

Visit Walker & Company's Web site at www.walkeryoungreaders.com

Printed in the United States of America

2   4   6   8   10   9   7   5   3   1

For Elly and Jules,
with thanks to the store detectives,
Kate, Sarah, and Ros

AISLE 1

"Price check on register three. Price check on register three."

Louisa looked up and down the aisle to make sure no one was watching. With her new Employee of the Month badge pinned to the front of her shirt like a bull's-eye drawn on her heart, she was an easy target. If anyone anywhere at any time wanted anything for any reason anyhow, she was the first person they would ask.

She'd been working out back when they made the announcement. "Could all available staff come to the staff lounge, please." When the manager hauled her up in front of everyone, Louisa thought she must be in trouble for leaving her coffee cup on the table. Louisa was already worn out from her night shift at the hospital, so when the manager told her she was Employee of the Month, she nearly cried. They gave her a plaque with a picture of someone standing on top of a mountain. *Out-*

standing effort, it said. *Some people dream of worthy accomplishments, while others stay awake and do them.* Stay awake? Was that all you had to do to be Employee of the Month? The manager presented Louisa with the bronze badge and pinned it to her shirt. He gave her two movie tickets and said "Well done, Louisa!" Then he told the other workers what a good example she was. Louisa didn't know where to look. Her hair was a mess and she hadn't cleaned her teeth properly. She stood there smiling like botched plastic surgery while they took a Polaroid photo and everyone clapped because they had to. *I'm gone*, she thought. *I'm a sitting duck.*

"*Price check on Register Three. Price check on Register Three, please!*"

According to the store manager, price checks were to be done by the nearest available staff member. Louisa was in aisle 1, at the far end, so someone else would have to do it. Badge or no badge. In the whole of the supermarket, there had to be another staff member who was closer to the registers.

Louisa repositioned the safety steps in front of the stationery and went on facing the shelves. Facing the shelves meant bringing the stock to the front, filling the empty spaces and making sure that the brand names were facing out. It also meant pulling out the garbage that customers had shoved back there: balls of chewing gum, old wrappers, and melted ice cream. You never knew what you would find.

She arranged the ballpoint pens according to their colors—blue, black, green, and red. She hung the paper clips back on their hooks. She brought forward the peel-and-seal envelopes. Good facing was more than just straightening the shelves. It required patience and an eye for symmetry. It was important to put the right products at eye level—the specials, the best sellers, and the promos—so that customers did not have to bend down too low or reach up too high. Louisa reached in and pulled out an empty soft-drink can. She finished stacking the packages of thumbtacks and the mini glue sticks. Out of habit, she put her hand in her pocket to check that her watch was still there. On the ward, a nurse's watch was used to measure the patient's pulse rate. A midwife used her watch to time the contractions of a pregnant woman and determine what stage of labor she was in. In the supermarket, Louisa didn't need a watch. In a supermarket it was all go, until someone told you to stop.

"Can I please have a grocery staff member to Register Three for a price check, PLEASE!"

"Okay, okay," Louisa murmured. "I'm on my way."

The girl on register three smiled at Louisa as if to say *Where the hell were you?* Her name was Chloe and she was always smiling. Cramped face muscles were an occupational hazard for the checkout girls. Even if your appendix had just burst, you were expected to smile politely at the customer. Even if the customer was a toothless bearded hag holding a blood-stained ax, you were expected to smile and ask them how they were.

Chloe handed Louisa a 60-watt lightbulb.

"It's broken," she said, glancing at Louisa's new badge. "Can you get another one?"

"I thought you said it was a price check."

"Does it matter?"

"But I was just there," Louisa protested.

Louisa was more senior than Chloe. She was the same age, but she had been working at the store for longer and had more responsibilities. In this situation, though, it made little difference. Louisa had to do what Chloe asked, and Chloe knew it.

"There are customers waiting," said Chloe, with the sweetest smile.

"I can see that," said Louisa.

The man at the end of the line shook his head and walked away. The remaining customers looked on impatiently.

"Don't worry," Chloe reassured them. "Louisa is our Employee of the Month!"

Louisa returned to aisle 1. She hadn't done the lightbulbs yet and the shelves were messy. There were pearl bulbs and clear bulbs, screw-in and bayonet types, all mixed together. She couldn't find the one she wanted. Standing beside her, an older lady was looking at batteries. When she saw Louisa's new badge, she smiled.

"You must be a good worker," she said. "Can you tell me, please, what is the difference between AA and AAA?"

"They're different sizes," said Louisa politely, continuing to search the shelves.

The lady nodded. "The trouble is," she said, "I don't remember which ones I'm supposed to get. They're for my grandson."

"I'm sorry I can't help you," said Louisa.

"I suggested he try those rechargeable batteries, but he said they weren't good enough."

"I'm sorry. I'm helping another customer at the moment."

The lady frowned. "But it's your job to help *all* of us, isn't it?"

This is a supermarket, thought Louisa, *not a nursing home.*

She found the bulb she was looking for, excused herself, and left.

At the end of the aisle, Jared and Dylan from the storeroom were wheeling a shopping cart stacked high with boxes. They were tall boys wearing white shirts that were too tight and black ties that were too short. When they saw Louisa coming, they stood to attention and saluted like soldiers.

"Stand back!"

"Look sharp!"

"Here comes the Employee of the Month!"

Louisa put her hands on her hips. "You guys aren't planning anything, are you?"

Jared and Dylan looked at each other. "Who? Us?"

"If anything happens to me," she warned them. "Anything at all . . ."

By the time she got back to the register, other customers had deserted the line and the one remaining woman looked furious. Before Louisa could give Chloe the lightbulb to scan, the customer grabbed it from her and shook it until it rattled.

"This one's broken, too!" she complained.

Louisa and Chloe looked at each other: *Because you just broke it!*

"They put a man on the moon," the woman scowled. "Surely someone could invent a better lightbulb."

I wish they'd put you on the moon, thought Louisa.

"There are other lightbulbs," she suggested. "But they're more expensive."

"Get me one, please," the woman demanded.

"Certainly, ma'am."

The shopping cart boys grinned as Louisa hurried past them again.

"Here she comes!"

"She never stops!"

"Get out of her way!"

"There goes the Employee of the Month!"

Back in aisle 1, a man had torn open a six-pack of toilet paper and was feeling its texture. When he saw Louisa coming, he quickly withdrew his hand and tried to close the packet.

"Just checking," he mumbled.

Louisa walked past him, trying to ignore the ripped packet. She began searching through the lightbulbs, but they all looked exactly the same. She rubbed her eyes and tried to focus. Hundred watt, seventy-five, sixty, forty . . . Before Louisa could find the one she was looking for, the toilet-paper man called out to her.

"Excuse me, miss! Can you help me?"

He glanced around to make sure that no one was listening.

"It's for my wife . . . She has . . ."

Louisa waited for him to finish.

"She's just had a baby."

"She has hemorrhoids?"

"Yes."

The man was blushing slightly, but Louisa wasn't embarrassed. She'd seen hemorrhoids. She had put on rubber gloves and asked patients to bend over while she examined them. It was all part of her nurse's training.

Louisa approached the shelf and picked out a roll of extra-soft toilet tissue.

"Try this one," she told him.

The man took the toilet paper gratefully and disappeared into the next aisle.

"Excuse me," said a familiar voice. "Which last longer, the double As or the triple As?"

Louisa knew it was no use trying to explain why it didn't matter which battery lasted longer.

"I don't know," she said, and shrugged.

Louisa listened wearily while the lady told her it wasn't good enough just to say *I don't know* and that she would have expected more from *someone like her*. In *her day*, the lady said, store clerks were there to assist the customers, not to be rude to them. In *her day*, people weren't in so much of a hurry.

In your day, thought Louisa, *people were dead by seventy*.

When the lady had finished talking, Louisa found a 60-watt, long-life, lightbulb and returned with it to the register. The woman in the line shook the bulb ferociously until she was satisfied, then gave it to Chloe to scan: $1.59

The woman shook her head.

"I'm not paying that much for a lightbulb. Do you think I'm stupid?"

Louisa and Chloe exchanged looks: *Yes. We do. We think you are very stupid, and we also think you are mean.*

When the customer had finally gone, Chloe turned off her light and put up a sign that said register closed.

"I'm on a break now," she said. "How about you?"

Louisa shook her head.

"Did you have a late night?" asked Chloe.

Louisa yawned and nodded.

"You bad girl," said Chloe.

Louisa had come home from her night shift at the hospital to find a stranger sitting on the couch with her mother. Blue suit. Orange mustache. Louisa's mom, Jackie, went to clubs a lot. She knew how to dress to attract a certain type of man—the desperate type. Jackie had introduced the man and he'd looked at Louisa in that odd way they all did. Louisa never listened when her mom said their names. What was the point in her knowing their names?

Louisa said nothing while Jackie told the man how proud she was that her daughter was going to be a nurse. She was thinking of going back to school herself, she said, although she hadn't decided what she wanted to study.

Yes, Mom, thought Louisa, *that's really going to happen.*

The man said something about how you're never too old to learn, which made her mom giggle, for some reason. Louisa went into her room and lay on her bed. Through the wall she could hear more giggling. Then the doorbell rang and a pizza delivery boy arrived. Her mom came into the bedroom looking for money. Louisa pulled out a twenty, and Jackie said she would definitely pay her back this time.

"When you get the money," said Louisa.

The pizza boy left and Jackie put on some music. It was the soundtrack of the movie *Chicago* and it made Louisa cringe to imagine her mother singing and dancing for the stranger. The lumps in his blue suit. The smile under his orange mustache.

Louisa was exhausted, but she couldn't sleep. At the hospital, a sixteen-year-old girl had overdosed in the bathroom, an hour after giving birth to her baby. Her newborn child was suffering from heroin withdrawal and would not stop screaming. As the young mother was leaving the room, she spat at the incubator, "That's not my damn baby!"

The soundtrack finished and for a while there was no sound from the living room. Louisa lay on her bed, waiting to see what would happen. The front door slammed and she heard the man swear as he got in his car. The toilet flushed, then Jackie came in and sat on the bed.

"You must think I'm awful," she sighed.

Louisa took her mother's hand. "It's okay, Mom. Go to sleep."

"Should I take a pill, do you think?"

"If you need to."

Jackie wiped a tear from her eye, leaving a smudge of black eyeliner on her cheek. "It was just a misunderstanding. I never meant to . . ."

"I know, Mom."

"It's just that . . . he seemed like such a nice man."

"It's what men do, Mom. They act nice."

Louisa waited until her mom was asleep, then she got up and did the dishes before the ants came. She turned off the stereo and put the *Chicago* soundtrack away. She took out the empty pizza box and put salt on the carpet where someone had spilled red wine. On the mantel, there was a photograph of her and her mother. Louisa hated it when people said how similar they looked.

"Behold! She walks amongst us!"

   "Once again, she has returned!"

   "She, who fears nothing."

   "She, to whom we all aspire."

   "The Employee . . ."

   ". . . of the Month!"

"Give me a break," Louisa pleaded.

She returned to her aisle to continue facing the shelves. She climbed the safety steps and stood there motionless. There was something wrong, but it took her a while to work out what it was. The Muzak had stopped playing. Above the silent hum of the air-conditioning, she heard the constant whispering of shoppers and carts in motion. *Should I go and change the tape*, she wondered, *or will someone else take care of it?* Louisa stood on the stepladder, trying to make up her mind. On the one hand, it was no big deal. The customers would survive without canned music. It was not a life-threatening situation. On the other hand, no one was doing anything about it. Was it possible that no one else noticed when the music stopped?

"Price check on Register Nine. Price check on Register Nine."

Louisa took out her watch to check the time. It took her a moment to realize it was upside down. As she reached up to restack the boxes of tissues, a piece of paper floated to the floor. A handwritten sign had been taped to her back.

It said, SLAVE.

She stood looking down at the sign, deciding whether or not to pick it up. *It's not fair*, she told herself. *Don't be such a baby*, she answered back. But it was too late. Weariness rose up and swamped Louisa like a wave. It washed away her sensible thoughts and flooded through her body. *What's the use?* she thought, as she slumped down on the top step of the ladder and softly began to cry.

AISLE 2

"Adam. Are you in there?"

Adam was drifting off when his father knocked on his bedroom door. Adam had a TV in his bedroom, which he left on out of habit. It was on in the morning when he woke up and still on in the afternoon when he came home from school. Adam's TV was like a faithful pet. It watched over him while he slept. It guarded his bedroom while he was out. And it kept his parents guessing: when it was on, which was always, they didn't know if he was at home or not.

Adam's parents said that too much lying around wasn't good for him, but Adam told them not to worry. "What about your homework?" they asked. Adam told his parents he didn't have any. But the truth was, his homework had been piling up for so long now that Adam could hardly bear to think about it. The pile had become a mountain, an endless high plateau that could never be crossed. In the end, Adam had no choice but to turn his back on it.

"Adam," his father called again. "Open up. I've got some good news."

Mostly, when anyone knocked on his bedroom door, Adam would lie there until they went away. Usually, when it was his father, the news was anything but good. Adam was needed to unload the dishwasher or put out the trash bins. It wasn't that these requests were unreasonable, it was just that they always came when Adam was busy doing something else, like watching TV.

Adam lay on his bed, listening to his father knocking. It was too late to open it now, he decided. If he opened the door now, his father would get angry and ask why he hadn't opened it sooner. "What were you doing in there?" "Why is the TV still on?" These were the kind of questions that Adam had no answers for.

But what if the good news really *was* good? He opened his eyes. What if a rich uncle had died and left him a massive fortune, or his number had come up in a million-dollar lottery? For a long time now, Adam had thought about getting a bigger TV and maybe a bigger bed, if only he had the money. He sat up. His father had stopped knocking, which in Adam's mind was *almost* proof that the good news was, actually, good. With an unprecedented burst of energy, he leaped out of bed, ran to the door, and unlocked it.

"Dad?"

"Good news," said his father. "I've found you a job."

The following day, instead of going home to watch *Looney Toons Blue Ribbon Classics* after school, Adam found himself standing in a linoleum passageway outside an open door marked MANAGER. A man in a suit was on the phone. He gestured for Adam to come in, but didn't try for any eye contact. Adam stood waiting, while the manager continued speaking into the phone. The room smelled of cigarette smoke. On the desk there was a monitor switching between different security cameras. A poster on the wall said

The 3 Ps of Professionalism—Punctuality, Presentation, and Politeness.

Adam had scored zero out of three for professionalism. He was late, his clothes were ratty, and he had his hands in his pockets. The manager was a friend of his father's, from the golf club. As a favor, he had offered to interview Adam for some part-time work. "A kick in the butt," his father had called it, "a taste of what's out there in the real world." Adam had told his father that he didn't want to work, and certainly not in a supermarket. "I don't have time," he said. "I've got my final exams coming up." But then his father got angry. "Graham is an important man," he said. "I told him you'd be there, and you will!" Adam had never seen his father get so pissed. Easier to go and do the interview badly, he decided, then he could go home and watch TV.

The manager put down the phone and extended his hand.

"Graham Powell," he said. "Have a seat."

The interview was very strange. Graham told Adam that his father was "top-notch" and "a magician with a sand wedge." He asked Adam all the usual questions and Adam tried to give the worst imaginable answers, without being too offensive or rude. Throughout the interview, the phone kept on ringing and Graham kept answering it. Adam got the feeling the manager wasn't even listening to him.

"Are you an enthusiastic, self-motivated person?"

"Not really, no."

"Why did you apply for this position?"

"Because my dad said he'd take away my TV."

"What are your strengths and weaknesses?"

"I like TV. I like having a good time."

"Any particular strengths?"

"Yeah. Like I said. Having a good time."

"Where do you see yourself in ten years?"

"Probably on a beach somewhere, soaking up the sun."

After the interview, Adam was introduced to Scott, the trainee manager who shook his hand and called him "bud." Scott gave Adam an aptitude test, which he really enjoyed doing. There were multiple-choice questions about counting money, telling the time and units of measurement. Following that, Adam was taken to the training room to watch videos on how to lift boxes, how to use a fire extinguisher, what to do if someone swallowed detergent, and the consequences of stealing from the till. Midway through the section on how to address customers, there was a long excerpt from the opening ceremony of the Sydney 2000 Olympics. Adam watched for ten minutes, thinking it must be some kind of motivational tape. But then it went to a commercial break and he realized someone must have taped over the training video.

At the end of it, Scott returned. He gave Adam a white shirt and a tie with the company logo on it.

"Congratulations, bud," he said. "You start on Monday."

At eight fifty-seven on Monday morning, with his shirt unironed and his tie left loose, Adam stood outside the supermarket waiting to go in. He was three minutes early, which was ridiculous, considering how hard he had tried to be late. He looked at the plastic bags blowing around the parking lot. There was broken glass everywhere and a shopping cart lying on its side. On the wall was an advertisement for a famous brand of running shoes. Underneath, someone had written the word *ANARCHY*, with a circle around the A. Adam knew what the word meant, more or less, but it wasn't something he had thought about much, until now. His comfortable lifestyle had been disrupted, but only temporarily. He had done what his father had asked him to do. He had gone to the interview and sat through the videos. He had got the job through no fault of his own, and now it was up to him to take control of his own destiny. Anarchy meant no laws. It meant chaos and disorder. Adam wasn't letting other people decide his future for him. Today, he was going to get himself fired.

The store manager was seated at his desk, as he had been the day before.

"Graham Powell," he said, shaking Adam's hand as if they had never met.

"I'm Adam," said Adam, just to be on the safe side.

Graham spun around in his chair, leaned down, and opened his bottom drawer.

"Adam, Adam," he repeated. "I've got you in here, somewhere."

There were dozens of name tags in the drawer, but none of them had his name on it. Graham sorted through them all. Then he picked one out and showed it to Adam. It said ANDY.

"How about you wear this one until we get yours made up?"

"But that's not my name," said Adam.

"Not a problem." Graham sounded slightly annoyed. "It's mainly for the customers, you realize."

Adam took the tag and pinned it to his shirt pocket. It was on an angle, but he didn't care.

"Any questions?" asked Graham. "Any concerns?"

It was a good opportunity to be rude, crude, stupid, or all three. But before Adam could say anything, Graham stood up and began shaking his hand again.

"Welcome aboard," he said. "Come and I'll introduce you to the sharks!"

He led Adam to a smaller room with four desks. There were two men and two women seated at the desks, and Graham introduced Adam to them, one by one: Nicola, the dairy manager; Cameron, the fruit manager; Amanda, the grocery manager; and Scott, the trainee manager, who said, "How are ya, bud?" as if he actually remembered him. Adam viewed each in turn, like changing channels on TV. Who would he have to offend, he wondered, and how, in order to be dismissed?

Amanda, the grocery manager, had short bleached hair. She was stocky, with strong arms and broad shoulders. Adam wondered if he could beat her in an arm wrestle and decided probably not. Would she have a short fuse? he wondered. Would she lose it, when he did what he had to do?

Amanda frowned at his name tag. "Andy?"

"It's not a problem," said Adam.

He followed Amanda to the end of the linoleum passageway. "This is the staff lounge," she said, showing him a room with a sink and a laminated table. "This is where you clock in," she said, stopping to enter his PIN at a machine on the wall. "This is Brian, the meat manager," she said, as a red-faced man tried crushing Adam's fingers with a handshake. "That was Stephen," she said, as they passed another worker without speaking. "And this is the cleaning cabinet."

Amanda opened the cabinet door. A horrible, moldering, primeval smell filled the air. It was as if the most unmentionably bad smells in the world had gotten together to do battle with the nastiest chemical smells, and the bad smells were winning.

Adam took a step backward as Amanda handed him a bucket and an old mop.

"Here you go. Now come with me."

Pushing the bucket on its wobbly wheels, Adam followed Amanda into the store. As a customer, Adam had thought of a supermarket as a place to visit briefly. Now that he was a worker, he saw it as a labyrinth with no way out.

Amanda turned the corner and he hurried to keep up with her. "This is aisle 2," she said. Aisle 2 was like a hardware store compressed into a single straight line. There was rat poison, superglue, padlocks, matches, steel wool, garbage bags, clothespins, and rubber gloves. The possibilities for anarchy were endless.

Halfway down the aisle, there were two yellow cones with *Caution/Slippery* written on them in big red letters.

Between the cones, Adam saw a pool of something black and sticky on the floor. It was impossible to say what it was or how long it had been there, but Adam knew what he had to do. Getting fired was not just a good idea. It had become an urgent priority.

"Not a problem," he murmured.

When Amanda was gone, Adam dipped the mop in the bucket. The handle felt slimy in his hands and the filthy gray water had floating chunks of milk in it. The wringer mechanism jammed so the mop stuck as Adam tried to squeeze it. He almost tipped the whole thing over. Spilling a bucket would not be enough, though, even if the water was disgusting. He would have to do something much worse to make sure he'd get fired. Adam imagined himself being chased down the aisles by Amanda and the other managers. He imagined the cheers of the shoppers and coworkers as they escorted him to the door. Then Graham would call his father and describe him as "terminally unemployable. The worse case I've seen." Mission accomplished. But how to make it happen?

The black substance was stuck to the floor like tar. It was too thick and viscous to remove with a mop. Whatever it was, it would be hard to get rid of. He looked up at the cleaning products on the shelves above him: ammonia, bleach, caustic soda, borax, scouring powder. There were all the brand names he had seen on TV: Mr. Clean, Clorox, Windex, Drāno, Comet, 20 Mule

Team Borax, Spic and Spam. One of them would be right for the job. And if he wasn't allowed to use them, even better. Why not do the job properly, with a squirt from all of them? Adam imagined the brief but passionate exchange he might have with Amanda. She would use words like *irresponsible* and *reckless*. He would use words like *freedom* and *dignity*. Then Amanda would march him off to see Graham, and that would be the end of it. He could go back to bed.

Adam got down on his hands and knees to inspect the mess more closely. Taking care not to dangle his tie in it, he lowered his head and sniffed. With his finger he touched the shiny surface and drew a large *A* for anarchy, inside a circle. It wasn't enough to land him in much trouble, but it was a start. Adam was kneeling there, deciding what to do next, when he heard the sound of someone softly crying in the next aisle. It was such an unexpected, foreign sound in that bright fluorescent place that Adam thought he must be imagining it.

The crying girl was seated on top of a stepladder in the next aisle. Her name tag said *Louisa*. She was pretty, he decided, for an Employee of the Month.

"Are you okay?"

Louisa looked up at him. "Are you new?"

Adam nodded as he took down a box of tissues from the shelf, ripped off the top, and offered her one.

"You're not allowed to, you know," said Louisa.

"What can they do?" said Adam defiantly. "Fire me on my first day?"

Louisa took a tissue and wiped her wet cheeks. "Probably."

Adam glanced at her badge again. She was very pretty—quite beautiful, in fact—for an Employee of the Month.

"Are you sure you're okay?"

"I'm just tired, that's all."

"Big night, eh?"

"Twins!" Louisa nodded.

Adam tried to imagine her dating two brothers on the same night. She really didn't look like the type.

"I'm training to be a midwife," Louisa explained.

Adam was relieved. "Do they pay you overtime at night?"

Louisa shook her head. "They don't pay me at all, but I don't care. It's what I want to do."

She smiled.

Her smile was what did it.

Adam was caught off guard. Deep inside of him, something was stirring. It was as if some hibernating creature had awakened at the end of a long cold winter and begun to crawl out of its log. The hibernating creature was Adam's soul and there was a light at the end of the log. It was a pretty girl with tear-stained cheeks who knew what she wanted to do with her life.

"How about you?" asked Louisa. "Are you still in school?"

Adam looked away from her, stalling for time. If he told Louisa he was still in high school, she would find out he was younger than she, which would not be good. But apart from going to school, there was nothing he actually *did*. The only "higher learning" he'd done was in TV documentaries.

"Next year," he said.

"You're taking this year off?"

"Kind of."

"It's so hard to choose, I know."

She was beautiful, happy, and caring. He was caught hook, line, and sinker.

"Nursing is such a good choice. It would be so great to have a job helping others." He was babbling now. He couldn't help it. "If I was a girl, I would definitely consider nursing."

"Guys do it too," said Louisa.

Adam felt the conversation slipping out of his grasp. He knew it was dangerously close to the edge.

"Guys can be nurses," he assured her. "But *midwives*, that's different. I mean, wouldn't it be a bit weird, having a guy deliver your baby?"

"The doctors who do it are mostly men," said Louisa.

"All the more reason," said Adam, "why midwives should be women."

Louisa laughed. "You don't really want to be a nurse, do you?"

Adam shook his head. "I guess not."

"I'd better get back to work," said Louisa. "Thanks, by the way."

"Not a problem," he said.

When Adam returned to aisle 2, Amanda was standing with her hands on her hips, staring at the black stain with the circled *A* for anarchy clearly visible. Judging from the look on her face, he was in trouble.

"Where have you been? I asked you to clean this up."

"I tried to," Adam mumbled.

"And this . . . this *A* symbol," she said. "Did you draw this?"

Adam knew if he answered yes, then that would be the end of his supermarket career. Saying it meant *A* for Adam or even *A* for Amanda would not work. They both knew it meant *A* for Anarchy. And anarchy meant no rules. It meant having no respect for authority and not doing what the boss asked you to.

"Are you going to fire me?" he asked.

"Do you want to be fired?"

Through a hole in the shelves, he saw Louisa climb down from her stepladder.

"Not really, no."

Amanda looked at Adam. Then, to his surprise, she laughed.

"Listen," she said, "to be fired from this job you'd have to run naked through the deli with a string of gourmet sausages hanging round your neck. You'd have to cover yourself in cream cheese and dangle a smoked trout between your legs. Even then, they'd just move you to the dairy section. Nobody gets fired from this place. You leave when you're ready to, or else when you die."

AISLE 3

"How are you today?"

"Fine thanks."

The man in the loose-knit woolen cardigan placed a small package on the counter. Chloe started the conveyor belt and watched the tampons make their way slowly toward her.

"Excuse me," said the man, politely. "Are those the right size for my girlfriend?"

Chloe looked at him closely to make sure he wasn't joking. She noticed his cardigan had a sailboat knitted into the design.

"I'm sure they'll be fine," she said as she picked up the package of tampons, size regular, and scanned it.

Chloe could tell a lot about a person, not just from what they wore, but also from the things they bought. It was a game she played to keep from getting bored. She would guess if they lived alone or how long they had been married, how many children they had and what kind of pets, how much TV they watched and what kind of garden they had, how rich they were and who they voted for. It was all there in what they bought, the quantity, and the brand name. You could never be completely certain, but a guy with 48 liters of Coke in his cart was either planning a soccer-team barbecue or else he was stockpiling weapons of mass destruction.

The cardigan man picked up his tampons and went home to his "regular" girlfriend. There were no more customers after him, so Chloe took a deep breath and lifted her chin. She placed her feet in a V and adjusted her neck and shoulders slightly to straighten her spine.

She was pretty enough, she knew, but not a natural beauty, the way some other girls were. (Her face, when she studied it closely, was not quite symmetrical.) Chloe had worked hard to make the most of what she'd been born with. She set herself high standards. (Her thighs and upper arms were nine-out-of-ten, but lately her butt had slumped to seven, an all-time low.) At the gym she imagined a machine that could stretch her DNA like rubber, and the generations of perfect offspring that might follow.

Like most of the staff, Chloe worked part-time. Full-time workers were entitled to overtime, plus additional leave and health benefits, so the company preferred not to employ them. Most of the other workers had plans.

Either they were still in school, or they were saving up to do something different. Chloe had dropped out of school for no reason, really. (A modeling agency had liked her portfolio, but so far there had been no work.) She wanted to be a dancer, but that was like saying you wanted to be a singer, a poet, or a movie star. One day, maybe. She wasn't planning to spend the rest of her life as a checkout chick, of course, but right now there was no other job available.

She had worked as a nanny once, for a wealthy family on the other side of town. The house was a palace and the children were little angels. Chloe couldn't believe it when she found out they'd had three different nannies in the past twelve months. The parents were polite and considerate, the pay was good, and the hours were fine. She had a nice room with its own bathroom. It was almost too good to be true. When Chloe asked why the previous nannies had all left, the children's mother said she honestly had no idea.

"We've just been very unlucky," she said.

Chloe felt her luck was beginning to turn.

Her next customer was a man in his early forties, maybe. One by one, Chloe scanned his groceries: *8 oz. smoked salmon, duck liver pâté, Couronne brie*. The guy was clearly loaded, but too old for her. Considering how income increased with a man's age, but *marriageability* decreased, the optimum age for a husband, she had decided, was twenty-eight. Chloe had figured it out. A few more flings here and there, until she met Mr. Right. Then it would be wedding bells and babies. If Mr. Right was loaded, having babies was a good career move. Like being a nanny, except with an early-retirement plan.

Who, or more important, *what* should Mr. Right be? A doctor would be good for when the kids got sick, but doctors worked long hours and were probably a bit "diagnostic" in bed. Marrying an accountant would be good for financial investments, but accountants were supposed to be a bit boring. An architect would design a stunning house for them to live in, but probably dress a bit cheesy. A lawyer would wear stylish suits and drive a flashy car, but the custody battle for the kids could get nasty if things didn't work out. A CEO would be loaded. They could live in a mansion and vacation in five-star hotels. Where she had worked as a nanny, the children's father had been the CEO of a big company. It was an important job, but he still had plenty of time for Chloe and the kids.

Chloe had been an excellent nanny: making bottles, changing diapers, singing songs, reading stories, and playing peek-a-boo. There was a toybox full of toys and a sandbox in the backyard. There was a housekeeper who came daily, so Chloe never had to clean or cook. The children were affectionate and well behaved. They called her "Lowie" and asked her for cuddles. She made them laugh and they made her feel like Mary Poppins. And while they slept, she was free to do what she liked. Chloe had settled in well and soon felt like part of the family. The children's father was charming and considerate. He brought home small gifts for Chloe and spoke to her more like a friend than an employee. After a month in the job, he told her about the family's plans to vacation in Hawaii and asked her to come with them, all expenses paid.

Chloe could have kissed him.

Thinking about her time as a nanny, Chloe felt a pang in her tummy. Not a pain, exactly, just an odd feeling, somewhere inside of her. Maybe she'd overdone it at the gym that morning. Or perhaps she was just hungry.

She looked at the magazines on the shelf opposite her register. The glossy covers boasting their Hollywood scandals: divorcées, sex addicts, big spenders, bankrupts, stars falling in love, stars falling out, stars making up, stars without makeup. And there were magazines about health and beauty with headlines about anorexia, bulimia, HIV, drug scares, virus scares, bacteria scares, vitamin scares, cancer scares, . . . and pregnancy scares.

Chloe felt strange, looking at those magazine covers. It was a light-headed feeling, putting her on the verge of tears. She placed her fingers against her tummy and breathed deeply in, then out again, to relax. Should she be doing fewer sit-ups? Was it something in her diet? Or had she pulled a muscle?

Surely she wasn't . . . she wouldn't be . . . because, after all, what were the chances . . . surely, she couldn't be . . . pregnant?

Chloe placed both hands against her belly and tried to imagine a tiny embryo growing inside her. Being pregnant would be the end of everything. A death sentence. She would lose her job. She would be unemployable. At the gym, they would laugh at her. Instead of body attack and kickboxing classes, she would have to switch to yoga and water aerobics with the older women. She would be tragically uncool. Her gym gear wouldn't fit her any more. She would be a single mother. She would have cellulite! She would never get a job as a dancer, not in a million years. And how could she ever meet Mr. Right if she already had a child? The Mr. Rights of this world weren't interested in other men's babies.

If she was pregnant—*if*—then who was the father?

It wasn't Gavin, the night manager. She and Gavin had "dated," if that's what you wanted to call it, but things fizzled out before they got too serious. Because Gavin worked nights, their one and only date had been hard to arrange. In the end, they had a picnic brunch together, then walked in the gardens and fed crusts to the swans. They rolled around on the grass in a clumsy, embarrassed way. (He was clumsy. She was embarrassed.) After that, Chloe had started doing Pilates and Gavin had fallen asleep. Sitting there, stretching her hamstrings and listening to him snore like an old man, it didn't feel like love. It felt like a marriage.

It wasn't Cameron, the fruit manager. She and Cameron had had something special. There was something between them that just clicked. They liked the same bands and the same movies. They ate the same food and agreed on almost everything. They talked. They laughed. They understood each other. Cameron told Chloe she was a special kind of girl—the kind you don't meet too often, he said. Chloe had fallen for Cameron in a big way. Things had gotten pretty intimate. They had messed around in his flashy sports car with the auto-reclining red leather seats. (She accidentally kicked his gearstick into overdrive.) But they had been especially careful, because the car was still new and Cameron was recently engaged to be married. The lucky girl.

And it wasn't Scott, the trainee manager. Chloe and Scott had had a thing, at least that's what Chloe thought it was. Scott had told her it was a thing, at least that's what she thought he said. Although he never actually used those words, he said. (Or at least later he denied it.) Scott and Chloe had tried talking about it. It wasn't that he didn't like her, he said. It wasn't that he didn't find her attractive. It was just that he wasn't ready yet, to make such a big commitment. Chloe told Scott she appreciated him being so honest. She understood, she said. It was just bad timing. But the truth was, she didn't understand it at all. It had certainly *felt* like a thing with Scott. Even though, in the end, it turned out to be nothing. Just like all the other times.

Guys were like lottery tickets, Chloe decided. They had *Your Chance to Win* written all over them. But when you scratched the surface, it always said *Bad Luck. Try Again.*

Chloe examined her fingernails as she replayed each date in detail. She thought about her coworkers and wondered if she could talk to any of them. Louisa, who was training to be a nurse, would be the right person, if only she wasn't so busy all the time. Chloe liked Louisa, but wasn't sure what would happen if she suddenly started pouring her heart out. Louisa was Employee of the Month, after all, and their breaks were only ten minutes long. There was Emma, on register 5, the brainiac who read big books and used intimidatingly big words. There was Rahel, on register 6, who wore a headscarf and a dress down to her feet. Chats about unwanted pregnancy? Not likely. There was Tessa, on 8 items or less, who was very tall (not that it mattered) and slightly spooky (which definitely did). There were the girls at Chloe's gym, of course, but all Chloe knew about them was what they ate for breakfast, how much they weighed, what brand of gym shoes they wore, and how many crunches they did. It was strange how many women she saw every day but never really talked to.

Guys were easy to talk to, but they really were like lottery tickets. (You had to be in it to win it.) If it wasn't Gavin or Cameron or Scott, then who?

The flight to Hawaii was leaving early the next morning. The family's bags were all packed and the children were asleep. It was late at night. The house was quiet. Chloe was taking a shower in her room. She was excited. She'd never been on an airplane before, and now here she was, flying first-class to the Waikiki Hilton. In the brochure it showed people lazing by the pool, and surfer boys in their knee-length boardshorts laughing with girls on the beach. Chloe had been to the tanning salon and forked out for a skimpy new bikini. She had done a double session at the gym that day to tone up her abs. Hawaii was so exotic and romantic. She could hardly believe she had been so lucky. She wanted to pinch herself to make sure she wasn't dreaming.

Chloe was imagining herself at a luau feast, dancing the hula with flowers around her neck, when the bathroom door opened. Through the steam and frosted glass, she saw the children's father standing there in his robe.

"Got room for one more?"

He was a man who was used to getting his own way. It was his house and his shower. He was her boss. He had been very generous. Instead of destroying the dream, it would all be so much easier just to go along with it. But Chloe couldn't.

"Get out of here!" she shouted.

The next morning, over breakfast, Chloe told them she was quitting. With the taxi still waiting outside, she sat quietly while the children cried and their mother screamed at her: *"How could you do this? You've ruined our vacation! What about the children?"* But even though she started to cry, Chloe refused to give her reason for leaving. If the three nannies before her had kept quiet, she wasn't going to be the one. She didn't want to destroy the family. She wouldn't do that to the kids.

Chloe looked up at the next customer in her line. He was wearing a sleeveless T-shirt and a small golden horn on a chain around his neck. He was grinning at her, too, in that way they sometimes did.

"Hello, Chloe," he said, reading the name tag pinned above her breast. "How are you today?"

"Fine, thanks."

The man with the horn placed a packet of condoms on the counter.

"What's your favorite flavor?" he asked.

Chloe looked him up and down. Late twenties. No muscle tone. A try-hard. He wasn't in her league.

"Banana," she replied. "What's yours?"

The man laughed but didn't answer. Then his face began to turn red. Chloe scanned the condoms and dropped them into the open plastic bag while he fumbled in his pocket for the money.

"Have a nice day," she said, as he took the bag and quickly disappeared.

Chloe adjusted her shoulder strap and flicked back her hair. What was it about her and men? she wondered.

CUSTOMER SERVICE

Louisa was working at the service counter. The sign above her head said: REFUNDS, INQUIRIES, FILM PROCESSING, CIGARETTES, FRESH FLOWERS. Adam watched her from a safe distance—the charming way she listened to the customers, the alluring way she tucked her hair behind one ear as she filled out the paperwork, the entrancing way she opened the register to refund their money. He watched her rearrange the flowers, fill the shelves with cigarettes, and empty out the garbage bin. Every little thing she did was magic.

Adam waited until there was no one else around before he approached the counter. He took a deep breath to calm his nerves. But when he tried to speak, no sound came out.

A pregnant woman pushed in with a cart full of TV dinners, cans of soup, disposable diapers, and large cans of formula. By the look of things, she was stockpiling for World War III.

"Give me a carton of cigarettes, please, dear."

Louisa turned to the shelves of cigarettes behind her. The packs all had warning signs like: SMOKING KILLS, SMOKING CAUSES HEART DISEASE, SMOKING CAUSES LUNG CANCER, SMOKING IS ADDICTIVE. Adam noticed that Louisa went out of her way to find one that said SMOKING WHEN PREGNANT HARMS YOUR BABY.

"Thanks, love."

When the woman was gone, Louisa looked at Adam.

"Hey there," she said.

Adam cleared his throat.

"Did you want something?" asked Louisa.

Adam nodded. There was something he wanted very much and he had put a lot of thought into how he should go about asking for it. For several days he had worked and reworked the wording of the one important question he needed to ask Louisa: *I was just wondering if you wanted to / would you like to / go out for a drink / a coffee / sometime? / someplace? / somewhere? / to get a bite / to grab something to eat / a meal / some food / I'm feeling pretty hungry and I just thought / when do you get off? / what time does your shift end? / If you were at all interested / would you consider? / If it's not too much to ask / I hope you don't think I'm rushing into it / don't take this the wrong way / would it be such a dumb idea if / what I'm saying is / do you? / would you like to go out with me?*

"I want you," he said.

"Excuse me." A nervous-looking man stepped up to the counter. "Do you sell bread?"

"Aisle eleven," said Louisa. "On your left."

"And butter?"

"Aisle seven, halfway down. You can't miss it."

Louisa looked back at Adam. Her face was so lovely, he could have cried.

"What was it you wanted?"

"I want you to go out with me."

The phone rang as he said it.

"Hang on," said Louisa as she picked it up. "Yes, we're open twenty-four hours, every day . . . No, we never close . . . Yes, we're open after midnight . . . Right through until the morning . . . Yes, we are open at seven a.m. because we never close . . . "

Louisa hung up the phone and looked at Adam.

"Did you say you were going out?"

Adam was rattled now. He had lost his nerve. How could he say what he wanted to say? How could he and Louisa even have a conversation with all these inter-ruptions?

"To the parking lot," he said hurriedly. "To bring in the shopping carts."

AISLE 4

With lightning reflexes, Jared lifted the transparent plastic door of the candy dispenser, allowed a single black jellybean to roll down the chute into his hand, and closed it again. He popped the jellybean into his mouth and quickly checked that no one was watching. The trick was to act normal and not draw any attention to yourself. After all, everyone stole candy, even the managers.

Farther along the aisle, Jared saw an elderly gentleman in a pin-striped suit take a soda bottle from the shelf. The man weighed the bottle in his hands. He looked at the label. Then, with a sudden twist of his bony wrist, he unscrewed the top.

Ffft!

The old man screwed the lid back on and carefully returned the bottle to the shelf. He took a step backward, nodding to himself. The corner of his mouth slowly creased into a smile. With his index finger waving up and down, he counted along the row of bottles. Then he chose another one and did the same again.

Fffft!

Grinning like a naughty little kid, he counted again, then downed a third bottle of soda. Holding it in both hands, he shook the bottle briefly, stopped, then shook it again. This time, he untwisted the top slowly to prevent it from spurting all over his suit.

FffffffShhhhhhh!

With a gurgle of pure delight, the old man returned the bottle to the shelf.

Jared stood watching in a kind of trance. It seemed so ridiculous, what the old guy was doing, you had to admire it. And there was something else that he couldn't quite figure. It was a feeling he hadn't felt for ages. Without waiting a moment longer, Jared took out his mobile phone and punched in an urgent message.

:) c u in #4 @$@p!!!!

Jared was an only child. As a baby, he had been constantly active and a very light sleeper. His mother saw it as a sign of his higher-than-average intelligence. His father said it was because she had spoiled him. *Would you like a red balloon, or would you like another color? Would you like ice cream or pudding or both? Would you like to turn off your light and go to sleep now, or would you like to stay up a bit longer?*

Jared's life was a long list of multiple-choice questions: (a) Yes, (b) No, (c) Maybe, or (d) All of the above.

From an early age, he had shown no interest in learning or interacting with other children. He was unable to concentrate on even the simplest task. At the dinner table he regularly threw his meals on the floor and only ever ate dessert. He had fallen out of his high chair several times, trying to climb up onto the table to eat the sugar. His father had given up shouting at him, and his mother avoided seeking medical advice in case it confirmed her greatest fear—that her son was autistic. But when Jared ran into a brick wall and broke his arm, the doctor diagnosed him as having attention deficit hyperactivity disorder and prescribed a mild amphetamine.

Jared took his medication twice daily with a lollipop. Gradually, he became quieter and less moody. At school, instead of crawling around under the desks, he sat in his seat and listened. Rather than fighting and throwing things at the other children, he began to make friends. Instead of ripping pages out of books, he was able to concentrate more on what he was doing. At the age of five, to his parents' great joy, Jared was cured.

Limping as he walked, but grinning from ear to ear, Dylan arrived within fifteen seconds.

"Hey, homey! What's happening?"

Jared made a fake hip-hop gesture with his hands. "Check it out, homeboy."

Dylan was Jared's best friend. The "homeboy" thing had started out as a joke but, like the hip-hop gesture, it was even funnier if no one laughed. According to Jared, only a real homeboy would say "homeboy" all the time, unless he was fooling the other homeboys.

Together, the two of them watched in awe as the soda man took down another bottle and untwisted the top with his bony fingers.

Fffffft!

"What's his game, homey?"

"Hard to say, homey."

"Who does he think he is? The soda inspector?"

"Who knows. Maybe he *is* the soda inspector."

"If he's the soda inspector, shouldn't he have a badge or something?"

"He could be working undercover."

"I seriously doubt that, homey."

"We don't want to jump to conclusions. That's all I'm saying."

Dylan looked at Jared. "Should we tell him to stop?"

Jared shook his head.

"The shelves never lie, dude. And besides, it's not our area."

As Jared got older, his hyperactivity slowly returned. At school, he was popular now, but constantly in trouble for disrupting the class. His parents received several letters from the principal: *Jared shows no concern for others . . . has no interest in the curriculum . . . his childish, self-indulgent behavior . . . sudden loud outbursts . . . physically threatening . . . constant fidgeting . . . disturbing utterances.* There was also a report from the school psychiatrist, recommending that Jared attend group counseling. But the thing that most concerned his parents was Jared's sleepwalking. Some nights, he would leave the house and walk toward the city, crossing busy roads with his eyes wide open. Once, they found him stomping on the neighbor's garden. Another time, he tried to suffocate his mother with a pillow.

Ffffft!

"He's past his use-by date."

"Did you know, homey, there are one-hundred-year-old tai chi masters who can catch a bullet with one hand?"

"What's your point?"

"You can't judge a book by its cover, homey. That's my point."

"But, homey, wouldn't the bullet pierce their skin?"

"Not if they're wearing metal gloves for protection."

"If that's the case, homey, it sounds like the metal gloves are what stops the bullet."

"I'm talking about tai chi masters. Watch and learn, homey. Learn from the master."

As Jared and Dylan stood reverently watching the old man, a worker came up and introduced himself. His badge said "Andy," but he told them his name was Adam and that this was his first week of work.

"What are you guys doing?" he asked.

"Working," said Dylan. "What's it look like?"

Another worker stopped to see what was going on.

"Andy, this is Andy," said Jared, introducing them.

"I'm Adam."

"My name is Abdi."

Each glanced at the other's name tag and nodded. Then, together, they all stood and stared at the old man.

Fffft!

"Should we tell someone, do you think?" asked Abdi.

"Fools rush in, homey," said Dylan.

"Should we get security?" said Adam.

"People in glass houses, homey," said Dylan.

"We can't just do nothing," said Abdi.

They all looked at Jared. But he just smiled and kept watching the old man.

Jared's first job was as a paperboy. His parents had bought him a twenty-one-speed bike with a multifunction speedometer and an aerodynamic helmet to cut down on wind resistance. Jared had set his alarm for five in the morning and leaped out of bed as soon as the first beep sounded. From the moment he left the house, he was racing against the clock, trying to achieve a new personal best. He modified his delivery route to make it more efficient. He rode with no hands, carrying two newspapers at a time. Jared was doing well, according to his own calculations, but then the newspaper began to receive complaints. People didn't like being awakened by the thud of a rolled-up newspaper slamming against their front door. They were sick of retrieving their paper from the branches of a tree or up on the roof. Finally, one of Jared's newspapers flew through an open window and broke a priceless vase. The insurance company said they would find a replacement, and so did the newspaper.

Jared was fired. According to his speedometer, he had ridden sixty-six miles, averaging an incredible seven mph!

Abdi approached the elderly gentleman cautiously.

"Excuse me, sir," he said. "Can I help you?"

The old man shook his head.

"Do you intend to purchase, sir? Or are you just looking?"

The old man grinned as he took down another bottle.

"I must inform you, sir, that customers are not allowed to open the products in the store."

The old man looked at Abdi and nodded.

"Please, sir. Give me that bottle."

But when Abdi held out his hand and tried to take it, the old man turned away.

"You are spoiling them for everyone else!" said Abdi. *Ffffft!*

After Jared lost his paper route, he tried his hand at cleaning car windshields. Each morning, during rush hour, he would set up at a busy intersection with a brush and a bucket of soapy water. When the traffic lights turned red, Jared would approach the drivers. Even if their cars were spotless and they clearly didn't want his services, he cleaned their windows anyway. Jared was fast. He could do ten cars before the lights had changed, and a couple more before the traffic began to move. But when he bent back the windshield wipers on a Porsche, the driver threatened legal action and said he would break both Jared's legs if he ever saw him again. Jared decided to reevaluate his options.

His next venture was a gardening business. Jared paid ten dollars for five hundred business cards, which he planned to hand-deliver to the mailboxes in his local area: SPEEDEE MOWING SERVICE. BUDGET RATES. NO JOB TOO LARGE OR SMALL. He had designed the cards on his computer. It was only after he got them back from the printer that Jared discovered the typo: SPEEDEE MOWING SERVICE. BLUDGET RATES. NO JOB TOO LARGE OR SMALL. Instead of getting the cards reprinted, Jared handed them out to his friends. They were a much bigger hit than the gardening business ever would have been.

Jared's behavior deteriorated. He was always getting in trouble at school, and at home he refused to speak to his parents, refused to answer their stupid questions, yes, no, or maybe. The school psychiatrist rediagnosed him as having bipolar disorder and wrote out a prescription for antidepressants. For years, Jared had gotten his amphetamines using an ongoing prescription with the same pharmacist. After switching to antidepressants, he simply found another pharmacist and began selling the amphetamines after school. With the money he made, Jared bought (a) speed and (b) alcohol which, combined with (c) the antidepressants, made him feel much better. Jared took antidepressants as if they were candy. On a bad day, he would pop two or three. Some days, he lost track of how many he had taken, but it didn't matter. The important thing was, Jared was cured again.

"I'm going to get the manager," said Abdi.

"I'll come with you," said Adam.

"You're making a mistake, homeys," said Dylan.

Jared had been silent. But as the two Andys began to walk away, he turned and gave them an intensely meaningful look.

"It's a can of worms," he said. "Once you open the can, that's it."

The Andys stopped and looked at him, trying to understand what he meant.

Jared shrugged. "Do what you like, homeys. But, sometimes, trying to fix things only makes them worse."

When the two Andys were gone, Dylan helped himself to a Mike and Ike and offered Jared one. The two of them had started work a year ago on the same day. They had helped each other in the aptitude test and taped over the training videos. Since then, they had always worked the same shift, unloading trucks and stacking boxes out in the store. When Jared came late or snuck off early, Dylan keyed his PIN and clocked him in or out. When Jared forgot his PIN, Dylan remembered it. When Jared fell asleep in the bathroom, it was Dylan who pounded on the door and woke him up. When Jared started laughing hysterically, Dylan grabbed his shirt and shook him until he stopped. When Jared said he felt like jumping in front of a train, Dylan laughed and called him a jerk. When Jared got angry and started breaking things, Dylan gave him caramels, gummy worms, licorice, jellybeans, taffies, and chocolates. In return, Jared sold Dylan amphetamines at 50 percent off the street price.

Fffft!

"What's the gas they put in soda, homey?"

Jared shrugged. "Carbon dioxide?"

"Is carbon dioxide dangerous in large quantities, do you think?"

"I'm pretty sure carbon *monoxide* is."

Dylan popped another Mike and Ike into his mouth.

"This is boring, homey," he said. "I've had enough."

Jared barely nodded as his friend limped away. He was still watching the soda man when he realized he had forgotten to take his pill that morning. He felt a flash of panic, but then he relaxed. After all, he didn't feel bad yet. In fact, he felt almost fine.

The soda man took down another bottle. He turned and grinned at Jared, and Jared grinned back. There was a flash of recognition between them. How many bottles had he opened? No one was counting. Why was he doing it? Who cared? Holding his neck in his hands, Jared rotated his head, untwisting it like a bottletop, releasing the pressure, letting it all come to the surface. He looked at the rows of candy dispensers, the bags of sweets hanging on their hooks, the chocolate bars in their colorful wrappers, and suddenly he felt wide awake. It was as if he'd been viewing his life through a window and now someone had taken the glass away. Everything was so sharp, so bright and so *real!* It was intense. There was so much to choose from, and Jared wanted all of it.

STAFF LOUNGE

"So what's he like?" asked Chloe.

"Who?" said Louisa.

Chloe rolled her eyes. "The new guy. Andy."

"We saw you," said Emma.

"His name is Adam," said Louisa.

"What were you talking about?" asked Chloe.

"Not much," said Louisa.

"It didn't look like that," said Emma.

"He looked pretty interested," said Chloe.

"He was just being friendly," said Louisa.

"I'm sure," said Emma.

"He seems like a nice guy," said Louisa.

"Not Chloe's type, then," said Emma.

"What's that supposed to mean?" Chloe demanded.

"He was just doing his job," said Louisa.

AISLE 5

Tessa could imagine her own funeral: a lonely little church on a long-forgotten hill; a cloudy, weepy sky; the wind softly moaning through the branches of dying trees; her family in the front row, dressed in black; her sisters crying. After the gloomy organ music, four faceless pallbearers would come and carry her coffin down the aisle, to the tumbledown graveyard outside. It would be like a wedding, Tessa decided, except the opposite.

"How are you today, sir?"

The boy in the line looked up at Tessa and scowled.

"Don't call me that," he mumbled.

Tessa smiled, because that was what you were supposed to do. She looked at the boy, with his shaved head and pierced lip. She looked at his long black coat and wondered if he was shoplifting.

"Sorry, *sir*," she said.

The boy stared at her blankly. There was no way of knowing what he was thinking. Tessa continued scanning his items, trying to ignore the rude way he was staring: herbal teabags, tofu, multigrain muesli, organic soy milk. There was no doubt about it. The guy was obviously a psycho.

"And no plastic bags," he added.

Tessa watched the boy put the groceries into his hemp shoulderbag. She smiled stiffly as he nodded and left. Her next customer was a lady with a shaved poodle in her cart. After her, there was a man who insisted on paying in dimes, then a woman with dried soap in her ears.

Why did the weirdos always end up in her line?

When at last there were no more customers, Tessa picked up a pen and began drawing a barcode on her palm, out of boredom. She swiped her barcoded hand across the scanner, but there was no reading.

What would it say? she wondered. *Girl, 50 percent Off.*

The cashiers were in the staff lounge, discussing Adam, the new worker. Tessa made herself a cup of coffee and sat down. She never knew what to say in girl conversations. She always felt clumsy and stupid, like an ugly stepsister trying to squeeze her big foot into a tiny glass slipper. While the others talked, Tessa flipped through the newspaper, pretending to read. She looked at the names in the death notices. There was an obituary about a nun who had lived in a convent all her life. Sister Lillian had been married to God, it said. She had never wanted children of her own. There was a photograph of Sister Lillian as a young woman. She looked happy enough, Tessa thought, but painfully shy.

Outside in the corridor, Jared and Dylan thundered past on their shopping cart. The other girls did their best to ignore them, but Tessa couldn't help smiling as she heard them take the corner too fast and thump into the wall.

Why did boys have all the fun?

By the time Tessa had finished her shift, the smaller shops were closing and the cleaners were clearing tables in the food court. The weirdo in the long black coat was sitting alone by the window, staring straight at her. Tessa looked away, then casually glanced back again, just to be sure. The strange boy nodded. It gave her a creepy feeling.

The sun went down behind a factory wall as Tessa headed for the bus stop. She wasn't comfortable in her work clothes. The fabric felt itchy against her skin and her shoes were pinching. Then she saw him again, still following her. Fear rose inside her. Instinct told her to run, even though she was taller than he was and there were still plenty of people around.

Instead, she walked to the busy street corner and stopped. If the boy went one way, she would go the other. And if he started to hassle her, she could get help from someone or wave down a passing car. To hide her nervousness, Tessa turned to confront him as he came toward her.

"What is your problem?" she demanded, when he had stopped right in front of her.

The boy reached into his coat pocket and for a moment Tessa thought he might pull out a knife. But then he gave her a pink piece of paper.

"We're having a party," he said softly. "Would you like to come?"

The invitation showed a picture of a circus fat lady.

Tessa was disgusted.

"Who the hell are you?" she blurted. "Do you think you're God's gift to women?"

Instead of looking offended, the stranger's face softened. When he laughed, it was gentle and unexpected.

"But I *am* a woman," she said.

When Tessa told her sisters she was going to a party, they teased her about what she would wear. Tessa never went to parties. She didn't own any makeup and she never did anything with her hair. While her sisters were playing with their dolls, Tessa was running around with the boys in the street. But at school, the same boys never let her join in with them, and because she was tall for her age, Tessa felt awkward among the girls. When the teacher asked the class what they wanted to be when they grew up, Tessa said "A fireman," and everyone laughed.

"I'm sure," said the teacher, "that Tessa would make a very good fire*person*."

"At least she won't need a ladder," someone snickered.

Ruby had said the party was very casual and that she should wear whatever she liked. So, despite her sisters' teasing, Tessa decided on jeans and a T-shirt. It wasn't very imaginative, but at least she would feel comfortable.

Instead of asking her dad for a lift, Tessa called a taxi and told the driver the address on the invitation. At first she thought there must have been a mistake. The house was a big, dark, rundown place in a street full of factories. It looked as though no one had lived there for years.

Tessa stepped over the broken gate. The front door was open and a candle flickered in the hall. She saw dark shapes of people in the candlelit rooms on either side: stretched out on the floor; playing African drums; demonstrating kung fu; wrestling a spray-painted dog. Tessa moved past the doorways like a shadow, through a crowded kitchen and up a creaking staircase.

Upstairs, there were closed doors and one big room with windows overlooking the street. People were leaning against the walls and a girl in a beanbag chair was having her hair braided. In the middle of the room was a table with dead candles, empty plates and bowls of cherry pits. Tessa went out on the balcony and looked down at the street below. A police car drove past slowly. She wondered how many people lived in the house and whether they paid rent. She wondered if any of them had jobs.

A guy with matted hair wanted a cigarette, but Tessa didn't have one.

"Have you seen Ruby?" she asked.

The guy shook his head. "Does she live here?"

"I think so."

The guy drifted away, leaving Tessa alone on the balcony. She was trying so hard not to be noticed that it took a while before she realized Ruby was standing beside her.

"Hey! You made it!"

In long earrings, Ruby looked much more like a girl.

"I didn't know what to wear," said Tessa. "I feel like such a nerd."

"Nerdy's okay," said Ruby.

"I think I'd better go. I'm no good at parties."

Ruby smiled. "If you *were* good at parties, I wouldn't have invited you to mine. But if you want to borrow any of my clothes, you're welcome."

"I should go."

"Come on," said Ruby, taking her hand.

She led Tessa down the hall to her candle-lit bedroom. There were cobwebs on the ceiling, a piece of silk pinned across the window, and a crack in the wall as wide as your thumb. There was a single mattress on the floor, a teacup and a pile of books without a bookshelf. From a small rack of clothes against the wall, Ruby picked out a black velvet dress.

"I don't usually wear dresses," said Tessa.

"Sure you do."

"But they make me feel so . . . girly."

"Girly is okay," said Ruby.

Tessa touched the material. "Are you sure it will fit me?"

Ruby held the dress up against her.

"It suits you," she said. "I think you should keep it."

Tessa smoothed the soft fabric.

"Why did you invite me? Why are you being so nice?"

"I thought you looked lonely."

"How would you know?"

"I've been lonely," said Ruby. "I know how it feels."

"I'm not lonely," said Tessa.

"You think no one understands you. It's the same thing, isn't it?"

"I am who I am. I can't change, just to suit others."

"That's what I like about you," said Ruby.

Tessa put on the dress and felt the cool velvet against her skin. She never wore dresses at home, but tonight she could be whoever she wanted to be. Ruby started dancing without music. She danced like a wasted raver, then a cosmic earth mother, keeping a straight face to make

Tessa laugh. They danced together, then to cool down they stood at the open window, feeling the night air on their faces and listening to the faraway sounds of the city. They saw a cat leap from one roof to another. They watched the moon find its way through a maze of clouds. Then, unexpectedly, Ruby leaned across and kissed her softly on the lips.

After that, they lay in Ruby's bed, talking about witches and how if they drowned they were innocent, but if they could swim they were burned alive. They talked about death and what would be the best way to go. Tessa wished it would happen unexpectedly: electrocuted by the toaster or hit by a falling branch. Ruby wanted it to be dramatic: struck down by an unknown virus, buried in a landslide, or attacked by a killer whale.

"Sometimes I imagine my own funeral," said Tessa.

"Do you ever speak to the spirits?"

Tessa shook her head.

"Would you like to?"

Ruby brought out an Ouija board marked with the letters of the alphabet and numbered from zero to nine. She lit a candle and turned out the light. She placed the teacup upside down on the board and the two of them touched it lightly with their fingers.

"Ask a question," said Ruby, "and the spirits will spell out the answers."

"Hello!" Tessa laughed. "Can you speak to us?"

They sat there, watching the candle and waiting patiently, then suddenly the glass began to move. Tessa was sure she wasn't pushing it and Ruby swore it wasn't her either. The glass moved slowly across the board and came to rest on the number *1*.

"What does it mean?" whispered Tessa.

"I have no idea."

The glass moved on, but it only ever stopped at numbers.

1 7 7 1 7 0 7 7 3 4

Then the candle went out, which, according to Ruby, meant the séance was over. Tessa wrote down the numbers. They made no sense, as far as she could see. If the spirits had gone to the trouble of moving the glass, why hadn't they spelled something out?

But Ruby, sitting opposite, had seen something Tessa hadn't.

"Look at them upside-down," she gasped.

When Tessa turned the numbers around, they said:

h E L L o L I L L I

On Monday, back at work, the cashiers were in the staff lounge. Chloe was telling Louisa and Emma about the hunky new instructor at her gym. When Tessa walked in, with her hair cut short and dyed blue-black, they took a minute to recognize her.

"I don't believe it!"

"Tessa?"

"Is that you?"

"My name is Lilli," she quietly informed them. "And I have come back from the dead!"

DELICATESSEN

Adam sat at his bedroom desk with his homework planner open in front of him. In the space where it said *SUBJECT / DATE DUE* he had written *PLAN B / NOW!* The desk was laid out with delicatessen food he had bought with a 10 percent staff discount. There were tubs of Greek olives, sun-dried tomatoes, Bulgarian goat's cheese, and Hungarian salami. It was good that Louisa was older, of course, in several ways that Adam could happily imagine. But it meant that Plan B—like the food from the deli—would need to be cosmopolitan and sophisticated, to show her how experienced and worldly he was.

Adam selected a piece of goat's cheese and popped it into his mouth. How would you milk a goat? he wondered.

On the TV there was an ad for a camera store sale. *Never to be repeated. Huge reductions on camcorders, SLRs,*

Polaroids, Instamatics, and digital cameras. Out they go! As Adam watched, suddenly the picture faded to a greeny-orange monochrome. He tried everything he knew to fix it, and when that didn't work he punched the set in frustration. The picture shrank to the size of a dot, then disappeared. Adam stared at the blank screen, not knowing what to do. Louisa was working at Customer Service, but he had no goods to exchange or questions to ask. He didn't smoke. He couldn't buy a bunch of flowers, then hand them back to her. For the rest of that night, without the TV to console him, he tossed and turned, unable to sleep. Finally, at daybreak, he came up with a brilliant idea.

AISLE 6

Careering down aisle 6 on an out-of-control shopping cart, Dylan's foot hit a packet of Mallo-mar cookies, which fell from the shelf before he could catch it.

"Whoa! Back up, homey!"

"Firing retro-rockets, now!"

Jared jumped from the cart and dragged it back the other way, crushing the cookies in the process.

"They're history, homey. Flat as a pancake."

"Flat as focaccia."

"Flat as a dead battery."

"Flat as a warm beer."

Steering the shopping cart piled high with empty boxes, they burst through the clear plastic doors and out into the storeroom, where Adam and Stephen were waiting for them. Maneuvering skillfully along the rows of unstacked pallets, Jared brought the cart to a halt beside "Goliath" the box crusher. Goliath was a relic from another age, battered and bruised by generations of store men. Adam watched Jared open the rusted orange metal doors. Inside was a solid block of crushed cardboard—a hundred boxes or more, compressed to the size of a case of beer.

"Getting it out can be a bit tricky," Dylan told Adam.

Jared grinned at Stephen. "You want to show him how we do it?"

Stephen was a pale boy with greasy hair and sideburns. "Not me." He shook his head.

"I'll give it a shot," said Adam.

The others stood watching while Adam wrestled with the dead weight of crushed cardboard. He pushed and pulled. He strained and heaved. He struggled and swore. The damn thing wouldn't budge.

"It's stuck," he said, wiping his sweaty forehead.

"You have to give it a kick," Jared instructed.

Adam kicked at the block until his foot hurt. He kicked with his other foot, then he kicked Goliath, just for good measure.

"Take it easy," Dylan warned him.

"It's hopeless," said Adam, exhausted.

"I told you," Stephen smirked.

"There's a trick to it," said Jared. "Watch and learn from the master."

Adam stood back while Dylan hung from the top of the box crusher and kicked at the cardboard block so violently that the storeroom walls began to rattle. There were very few workers who had the strength or the nerve to do this job, but because of the metal pin through his right ankle, combined with the loss of feeling in his foot, Dylan was one of them.

"Nice work," said Jared, when the block had fallen to the floor with a heavy thud.

Dylan rested his foot on it, like a big-game hunter. "You know how cardboard comes from paper, and paper comes from trees?"

"Everybody knows that, homey."

"Well, it just occurred to me, where do trees come from?"

"They come from the ground, homey."

"Sure, trees come from the ground, but they're not made out of dirt. So, like, where do they *come from*?"

"That's a botanical question, homey. I'm sure there's a simple explanation."

Adam and Stephen both shrugged and shook their heads.

"Think about it," said Dylan. "Trees are just nature's way of turning dirt into cardboard boxes."

Jared thought about it. "Interesting angle, homey . . . You ready?"

"Willing and able."

Adam and Stephen watched as Jared and Dylan began their assault on the boxes. Like soccer players, they passed and kicked them. Like dancers in a modern ballet, they stomped and pirouetted, treading each box down flat before throwing it into the crusher. The job was almost done. A single V8 vegetable juice carton to go. When Dylan went to stomp it, somehow his foot got stuck inside. He raised his leg and tried to shake it off, but the box had bent into the shape of his shoe and wouldn't move. Dylan went rigid.

"You okay?" Jared asked.

"He looks like Han Solo, flash-frozen in carbonite," smirked Stephen.

Adam started laughing, but when he saw Dylan's face, he stopped.

"Hey, homey," said Jared. "Are you all right?"

Dylan didn't answer. His face was a mask, and his mouth hung open, as if he had just seen a ghost.

Dylan's family owned a motor repair business. His older brother, Phil, worked for their father as an apprentice mechanic. It was Phil's job to wash the engine parts, clean the benches, and help with services and minor repairs. Phil was a good worker, but he and the old man were always arguing about new technology versus time-honored traditions. Sometimes the arguments got heated. The two of them would stand there, face to face, each refusing to back down. Phil would threaten to quit, then storm off to the bar to curse the ignorant old fool and his dumb, backward ways. He always came back.

Dylan had never trusted Phil. When they were kids, Phil ignored Dylan, as if he was a stranger. Then, after Phil started working with the old man, Dylan hardly saw him any more. His big brother was little more than a scribbled name inside the covers of his hand-me-down textbooks. It was Dylan's ambition to go further in school, to learn more than his brother had, and to write his own name on the unmarked pages of new textbooks. But when Dylan's friend Jared started selling amphetamines, it wasn't long before Phil heard about it. Not only did Dylan's big brother become a regular customer overnight, he also became Dylan's best friend.

There was one job that had been a huge source of conflict between Phil and the old man. For his eighteenth birthday, Phil had been given the family car. Phil had big plans for the Mustang. He wanted to take out the straight six-cylinder engine and put in a V-8. He wanted fat tires, chrome wheels, and chrome tailpipes. He wanted to lift the hood and lower the front suspension. In Phil's head, the Mustang was all set to be the greatest babe-mobile ever. But the old man wouldn't have it.

"You can't put a V-8 engine into that car," he said. "It just won't go."

Phil showed him the drawings, and they argued about it. The old man explained that a V-8 Mustang was totally different under the hood, and that insurance premiums increased with engine size. Phil showed the old man the mounting blocks designed to his personal specifications and said he couldn't care less about insurance premiums. The old man said he didn't care whose car it was. He wasn't letting Phil do it in his workshop, especially since he wasn't even a qualified mechanic yet.

So Phil went down to the bar and got drunk again with his friends.

"I'll show the old bastard," he told them.

Eventually, Phil found the V-8 engine he was looking for. He had it tested and oil-bathed, then he waited for a weekend when their parents were away. Bright and early on that Saturday morning, he had the new engine delivered to the workshop. He and Dylan unloaded it with the hydraulic floor crane and set it down on wooden blocks. When the delivery truck had gone, Phil rolled down the garage door and padlocked it. From his toolbox he produced a bag of white powder he had specially bought for the occasion. It was speed, Dylan knew; enough to start an elephant stampede.

All that day and on into the night, the two of them worked on the car. First, they used a block and tackle to get the old engine out. Dylan wondered if the chain was strong enough to lift it, but Phil said it didn't matter. The straight six was just a piece of junk, anyway. With the engine removed, they put the Mustang up on the big hoist. When Dylan checked the supports to make sure they were holding the car safely, he noticed that two were off-center. He showed his brother, but Phil assured him it was OK.

"Look!" he laughed, pushing the Up and Down buttons, making the car jerk around on the hoist. "Steady as a rock."

The two of them got in under the car to change the mounting blocks. Dylan calculated the dead weight of the chassis, its large mass times the force of gravity, suspended above his head. He imagined the forces in equilibrium, the change in kinetic energy, the principle of moments and the stresses they must be generating in the T-frame of the hoist. He thought about the hydraulic lifting system and the explosive pressure of the compressed oil inside each cylinder.

His brother was working intensely now, asking for tools and straining silently until the veins stood out on his oil-stained arms and hands. "Shifter . . . Not that one, the big one. Torque wrench . . . Get me another beer."

When the new blocks were finally bolted into place, they lowered the hoist until the car was on its four wheels again. Next, they rolled in the floor crane, with the new engine swinging from side to side. Dylan wondered about the tension in the chain, the forces inside each individual link and the molecular structure of steel as they moved it into position, making sure that everything lined up. He pulled his hands out just in time, as Phil released the hydraulics, letting the engine drop down with a clunk.

It didn't fit.

Phil took a break to assess the situation, chugging beer, cursing and shoveling handfuls of chips into his mouth. They were running out of time.

They took out the new engine and put the car up on the hoist again. They unbolted the mounting blocks and redrilled the holes. Phil was working in a frenzy now, sniffing and mumbling and rubbing his eyes to stay awake. It was the old man's fault for having such lousy tools. It was the old man's fault that the business was losing customers. If his old man couldn't get with the times, Phil would have to get out and start his own business. Who knows, maybe one day the old man would end up working for him!

Dylan looked at the floor of the workshop, covered in discarded tools, empty beer cans and crushed potato chips. He wondered what the old man would say if he walked in the door right now.

When the modified blocks were in place, they tried to lower the engine again. It wouldn't go until Phil got out a mallet and furiously hammered the blocks into shape. He banged his knuckles and tore off a layer of skin. But instead of stopping to bandage his hand, he wrapped it in a dirty handkerchief and kept going.

By now, it was Sunday afternoon. Neither of them had slept or eaten a healthy meal. The bag of speed was empty and Phil was a nervous wreck. He wouldn't stop cursing and swearing, blaming Dylan for wasting his time and giving him the wrong tools.

"What the hell was I thinking, trying to do this on my own? What's the point of you even being here, when you're so useless?"

"Do you want me to leave?"

"You're not going anywhere until we're done."

Finally, the new engine was in place. It took them another several hours to connect it all up. By the time they were done, it was Sunday evening and getting dark outside. The plan was to take it out for a test run. If all went well, they would come back and weld the new mounting blocks permanently into place. The old man would arrive at work the next day, and when he saw the Mustang with its new V-8 engine, he couldn't help but be impressed.

When everything was ready, Phil got behind the wheel and turned the key in the ignition. The car started nicely, then he gave Dylan the thumbs up through his blood-stained handkerchief.

"Let's go," he said.

The street ahead was empty so Phil pressed the pedal flat to the floor. The big V-8 engine roared as the car accelerated. From the horrible smell of smoke and the grinding metal noise, Dylan knew they had burnt the clutch to hell. They would need new plates and a gearbox, but Phil hardly noticed. He was beyond exhaustion and way past caring. Nothing could stop him now.

Force equals mass times acceleration. Momentum equals mass times velocity. There was a stop sign ahead of them, but they were going too fast. Dylan grabbed hold of the dashboard as Phil slammed on the brakes. The car skidded. There was nothing he could do to control it. The principles of motion and the laws of kinetic energy were unchanged. The car hit the corner lamppost with such an impact that the engine came free of its mountings and was pushed back into their unprotected legs.

"Dylan! Are you okay?"

As Dylan stood motionless with his foot stuck in the cardboard box, the terror of that moment came flooding back. Twelve months after the accident, his body had more or less recovered. The pin in his ankle was made of titanium alloy and held in place by twelve screws going into the bone. Dylan had lost all feeling below his right knee and would never be able to drive a normal car. But after months of painkillers and physical therapy, at least he could walk with a limp. It was more than his brother would ever do.

Both Phil's legs were crushed. In the surgeon's opinion, Dylan's brother was lucky to be alive, but twelve months after the accident, Phil still wished he were dead.

"Dylan. Can you hear me?"

Jared stepped up to face his friend. He ripped the cardboard box from Dylan's foot. Then, with his hands on Dylan's shoulders, he spoke calmly.

"You told me how it was. The flashing red lights, flashing blue lights. The sound of tearing metal as they ripped the car apart to get you out."

"And the screaming," Dylan murmured.

Jared nodded. "You said that Phil was screaming."

"He wouldn't shut up," Dylan smiled grimly. "It just got louder and louder, until I couldn't tell the difference between the screaming and the grinding metal. I couldn't move. I couldn't get away from the noise."

"That's when you lost it," said Jared.

Dylan closed his eyes. "I started hitting Phil, just to get him to shut up. I was laying into him and abusing him. I was out of control, until I realized he wasn't reacting. Phil was unconscious. He wasn't the one who was screaming. . . . It was me."

CUSTOMER SERVICE

Louisa was doing her best to explain to the irate man in the tortoiseshell glasses that his item could not be exchanged.

"What's the point of calling it Long Life Milk," said the man, "if it spoils?"

Louisa showed the customer the expiration date, clearly stamped on the side of the box. The man took the box and held it very closely as he read. Then he looked at Louisa.

"I'm not blind. I thought '08' referred to the year, not the month."

Louisa shook her head.

"It's Long Life," she said dryly. "That doesn't mean it's *eternal*."

The man glanced at her badge. "I don't care who you are. I'm not about to be pushed around by a cashier! Either you give me a refund or henceforth I will buy my groceries *elsewhere*."

Louisa gave him his refund. She hadn't meant to answer back like that, but she hadn't had much sleep and, anyway, the guy was asking for it. All week, Louisa had been working the night shift in the emergency ward. The traumas and injuries she had seen made customers' complaints seem trivial by comparison. Comatose patients didn't care when the milk went sour.

On the form, where it said REASON FOR REFUND, she wrote: *Customer needs a reality check.*

When Louisa looked up, Adam was standing at the counter, wearing casual clothes and sunglasses.

"Hey there," he nodded, taking off his sunglasses and hanging them from the unbuttoned collar of his shirt. "I'm not supposed to work today, as you probably know or might have guessed."

Louisa stared at him. There was something strange about the way he was talking and he was dressed like a middle-aged man.

"What are you doing here?"

"I was out this way. I thought I'd just, you know, swing on by, to check out what was happening."

The phone rang. "Hold the line, please," said Louisa, transferring the call.

Adam nodded at the buckets of fresh flowers. "What are those blue ones called?"

"Irises. Did you want to buy some?"

"Do you like irises?"

"They're okay." Louisa shrugged.

Adam unhooked his sunglasses and began polishing them on his shirtsleeve.

"Another day, maybe. I'm on my way into town. To the art gallery, actually."

"Alone?"

"Just me."

"What's there?"

Adam's face dropped. "What do you mean?"

"Is there an exhibition?"

"Hopefully. Probably. I mean, I'm sure there will be something."

Louisa looked at the irises. "I went to the Van Gogh. Did you see that?"

Adam stared at her blankly.

"Some people say Van 'Goff,'" she added. "He was a brilliant painter, but so tormented. Did you know, he cut off his ear and sent it to his girlfriend?"

Adam was shocked. "Why would he do that?"

"It was probably just one of those things," said Louisa. "*I want to be with you, but you don't want to be with me.*"

"How do you know?"

"All I'm saying is, perhaps they were friends, but she didn't think of him in *that* way."

"Maybe all he wanted was a bit more of her time?"

Louisa grinned. "A sympathetic ear, you mean?"

Adam frowned. "Didn't she realize what he was going through?"

"I'm sure she felt bad."

"Not as bad as he did."

"Obviously."

Adam tugged on his earlobe. "I hope they worked it out, in the end."

"Actually, he killed himself."

The phone rang again. "Front desk," Louisa replied. "If the card won't swipe, you have to delete the transaction. Do you know how to do that? Hang on, I'll come over."

Adam knew that Louisa was busy. He didn't mind, though. He had come prepared.

"Just before you go," he dug his hand into his back pocket and pulled out a roll of film, "could you send these off to be developed?"

AISLE 7

SCENE 1: *Emma is speaking on the phone*

Emma

"I'm sorry I haven't had a chance to call you, Mom. I've been so busy . . . Work's fine. They've asked me to work overtime during the holidays . . . Because I need the money, Mom . . . Yeah. The college is pretty empty. Our grades aren't up yet . . . I know they'll mail them out, but I want to see how my friends did . . . It's summer, Mom. Everyone goes to the beach . . . No one's even heard of Terlingua . . . Because it's so far away, of course . . . I *do* miss you, and Dad . . . How are the calves? Are they getting bigger? . . . Because I've been busy . . . I'm learning my lines for the next production . . . *Henry IV* . . . No, not Shakespeare. It's by Luigi Pirandello . . . Actually, he's quite famous, Mother . . . It's about a man who falls off a horse and forgets who he is . . . It's too complicated to explain . . . Well, he's an actor who's supposed to be playing the title role, but after the accident he believes he actually *is* the king. Everyone plays along, just to humor him, so in the end you don't really know if you're watching a play or not . . . No, Mom. It's not out on video . . . Because that's the whole point. It's like *Hamlet*. It's a play within a play. 'All the world's a stage' . . . No, that was another play . . . Of course I do . . . I hope so too . . . I'll try to get some time off, I promise . . . Yes, Mom, I'll *really* try."

SCENE 2: *Two boys are standing at Emma's register*

First boy
Hey, Emma! I didn't know you worked here.

Emma
I didn't know you shopped here.

Second boy
We haven't seen you for a while.

First boy
We thought you'd dropped out.

Emma
Actually, I've been rehearsing a play.

Second boy
We were just, like, picking up a few things for tonight's party.

First boy

Any chance of a discount?

Emma

Sorry. I'd love to, but I can't.

Second boy

What happens if you, like, forget to swipe something? Isn't that the same thing?

Emma

Except I could lose my job.

First boy

Come on, Emma. No one's around.

Emma

There are cameras, you know.

Second boy [looking up at the ceiling]

I can't see any.

First boy

Don't worry, Emma. We'll take the rap. We won't turn you in.

Second boy

Even if they, like, torture us or give us a lie-detector test.

Emma [laughs]

I'm sorry. I'd *really* love to. But alas! I cannot.
[The boys pay, then leave.]

Louisa [watching from the service counter]
What was that all about?

Emma
Just some boys from my college.

Tessa [serving at the next register]
You shouldn't let them push you around like that.

Emma
They weren't pushing me around, Tessa. Boys can be quite cool, you know.

Tessa
What's that supposed to mean?

Emma
It means, I don't have a problem with boys, that's all.

Tessa
If you've got something to tell me, Emma, you should just come out and say it.

Louisa [tactfully]
Anyway, I'm glad you didn't do it. Management would have found out, for sure.

They're really cracking down. Has Graham spoken to you yet?

Emma
Not yet.

Tessa

I saw him yesterday.

Louisa

What sort of things did he ask you about?

Tessa

Just the obvious. Had anyone been acting suspiciously? Had I seen anyone milking the till or forgetting to scan the items?

Louisa

What did you say?

Tessa

I told him to mind his own business. I told him I thought only the police were allowed to interrogate people.

Emma [sarcastically]

That was courageous of you.

Tessa

You know how it is, Emma. There isn't a single worker in this place with a perfect record. Management included.

Emma

Do you think Graham would fire us all?

Louisa

He's the boss. I guess he can do what he wants.

SCENE 3: *Louisa leaves to return some items to the shelves. When Tessa takes a break, Chloe replaces her at the register*

Emma

Did you ever see *Survivor*?

Chloe

I saw the first season.

Emma

I mean, would you ever do something like that?

Chloe

For a million dollars, I'd do just about anything. Wouldn't you?

Emma

You only get a million dollars if you win, remember. It wouldn't be easy.

Chloe

You'd have to be good at making friends.

Emma

And totally ruthless when it came to getting rid of them.

Chloe

You'd have to get used to the cameras, too.

Emma [looking up at the roof]

That would be easy enough, for us.

Chloe

You'd have to act as if you cared, even when you were stabbing someone in the back.

Emma

You'd need to be stoic and resolute, so that no one could guess how vulnerable you felt.

Chloe

It's supposed to be reality TV. But really they're just like actors.

Emma [nods]

They sure know how to milk it, don't they?

Chloe [looking up at the ceiling]

Do you think Graham actually watches us?

Emma

He probably has nothing better to do.

Chloe

Do you think he ever sees anything?

Emma

You mean, someone forgetting to scan items?

Chloe

Everyone does it, don't they?

Emma [smiles]

No one's perfect. And accidents do happen, I guess.

Chloe [smiles]

Especially when we're busy.

Emma

Would he ever fire anyone, do you think?

Chloe

Not without any evidence.

Emma

But someone might turn us in, to avoid getting fired themselves.

Chloe

And Graham would have to do it, as a warning to the rest of us.

Emma

So instead of waiting for someone else to betray us. . .

Chloe

. . . we should do it first.

Emma

It would be like voting someone out, the way they do on *Survivor*.

Chloe

The tribe has spoken!

SCENE 4: *The next day. Emma is in the staff lounge.*

Tessa [enters]

Did you rat on me, Emma?

Emma

I have no idea what you mean.

Tessa

Don't look so surprised, Emma. Graham accused me of stealing, then he told me to get my things and leave.

Emma

That's terrible! You poor thing!

Tessa

I asked him to show me the proof, but he said it was none of my business. That's when I knew someone must have turned me in. And I'm pretty sure it was either you or Chloe. Because I know you both hate me.

Emma

That's not true.

Tessa

Yes it is, Emma. You hate me because I don't dress like you, and because I don't go all stupid whenever boys are around. You're a backstabber, Emma! I know it!

Emma [upset]

That's unfair, Tessa! I'm not like Chloe. I don't demean myself in front of boys. And I don't hate you the way

Chloe does. If anyone was going to deceive you, Tessa, it would be her, not me. Just yesterday, she said . . .

Chloe [enters]

Hey guys! What's up?

[Emma looks away]

Tessa

I just got fired, Chloe. And Emma was in the middle of telling me who she thought might have told on me. Weren't you, Emma?

Emma [embarrassed]

I was just . . . I didn't mean . . .

Tessa

Come on, Emma. I'm sure you don't mind if Chloe hears. She's a good friend of yours, isn't she?

Chloe

What was it, Emma?

[Emma buries her face in her hands, doesn't answer]

Tessa

Are you going to tell her, Emma? Or shall I?

Chloe

Tell me, Emma.

Tessa

She can't tell you, Chloe, because she . . .

Emma

Okay. Okay. You win.

Chloe

What's going on?

Tessa

Emma said it was you, Chloe. That you were the one who—

Emma [tears rolling down her cheeks]

It wasn't Chloe. It was me. I don't know how it happened. Sometimes I say things just to make people happy. I tell people what they want to hear. Graham asked me, so I told him. [sniff] How could I say no? I'm so ashamed. I feel so stupid. [sob] I'm not a bad person. I'm sorry, Tessa. [sob] I just made a mistake, that's all.

Tessa [softer]

Anyway, I don't care. I'm sick of this place. I don't want to work here anymore.

You've probably done me a favor, Emma.

[Tessa exits]

Chloe

I hope you're satisfied, Emma.

[Chloe exits]

[When Tessa and Chloe have gone, Emma wipes her eyes and takes a deep breath. She imagines a curtain closing, then opening again. As the audience rises to give her a standing ovation, she takes a step forward and bows]

CUSTOMER SERVICE

"Are my photos back yet?"

"What name was that?" Louisa teased.

"They're under A for anarchy," Adam smiled.

Louisa sorted through the envelopes until she found Adam's. He paid her the money and she handed it to him.

"Don't you need to check them?" he asked.

"What for?"

"At the photo shop they check the prints to make sure the customer is satisfied."

"You could always return them, if you're not happy."

"Because I experiment with light," said Adam, proceeding to lay the prints out on the counter, "my work can be a bit tricky to develop." He started to explain about apertures and shutter speeds, but stopped himself. Plan B, after all, was to *show* Louisa how cosmopolitan and sophisticated he was.

Louisa looked at the photos laid out in front of her.

There was Adam reading a newspaper in a sidewalk cafe, Adam standing reflected beside a river, and Adam silhouetted against a factory wall. There were photos of broken glass and burned-out cars, of graffitied trains and vandalized phone booths. Since his TV had been sent off to be repaired, Adam had been getting out of the house a lot more.

"Hmm." Louisa nodded. "A couple of good ones in there."

"If there's one you really like, I could get a reprint."

Louisa scanned the photos. Was she interested in anarchy, Adam wondered, or was she interested in him? Louisa picked out the photo of him standing by the river. Adam's heart began to race. After all, he did look very thoughtful and interesting in it.

"How did you take this?" Louisa asked.

"Automatic timer."

"What's that in the background?"

When Adam looked closer at the photo, his heart sank. "It's probably just some garbage," he said, gathernig up the prints and putting them back in the envelope.

"It looks like a bag."

"Terrible, what some people leave lying around."

"It's a backpack."

"I should be getting back to work," he said, taking the photo.

As Adam walked away, the phone rang at the service desk.

He heard Louisa speak into the microphone. "*Adam, to the front desk. I mean, Amanda.*" She quickly corrected herself. "*Telephone for Amanda, at the front desk.*"

On the way out to the storeroom, he threw the photos in the trash.

AISLE 8

Jared and Dylan had gone into "babe alert," following the platinum blond at a not-so-discreet distance while pretending to stock the shelves. Her shorts were very short and her halter top was chosen to show off her tan. She wore eyeliner like Cleopatra, pale pink lipstick, and matching nail polish. In her knee-length boots, her denim hat and matching shoulder bag, she looked more like an MTV presenter than a supermarket shopper.

Rahel and Brian, the meat manager, stood watching from the butcher's window at the back of the store.

"Does she know she's being followed?" asked Brian.

"I'm sure she does," said Rahel.

"Do you think she needs some assistance?"

Rahel looked at Brian's apron. "You'd better wipe that blood off first."

"Look more sophisticated, you think?" Brian raised one eyebrow.

Rahel tried to keep a straight face. "Definitely."

Brian was a man of few words. For twenty years he had worked in a slaughterhouse, standing for eight hours a day up to his ankles in a river of blood and gore. Brian had slaughtered sheep, cows, and pigs. He'd skinned them and trimmed the fat. He had disemboweled their carcasses and sorted the steaming organs with his bare hands. For half his life, Brian had cut, chopped, and lifted meat. On his arms were scars from accidental knife wounds. His back was gone, and most days it hurt just to sit. When Brian had asked Rahel if she was interested in taking the job, he didn't beat around the bush.

"Can you handle the smell?" he asked.

"I think I can," Rahel nodded.

Rahel had done her time on the registers. She was tired of the way the customers always looked at her headscarves and long dresses as if she were a slave from a Third World documentary.

"There's not a lot to it," he said. "Mostly, you'll be weighing and pricing the meat."

"I'll give it a go," she said.

Rahel went home that night intending to tell her father that she would be working with unblessed meat, including pork. She wasn't actually butchering it, and her father was open-minded. Rahel hoped he would see it from her point of view.

Rahel helped her mother cook the evening meal. When the family had eaten, she washed the dishes, then helped her younger brothers with their homework. After the boys had finally gone to bed, Rahel sat down with her parents. But before she had a chance to speak, her father announced that he had some important news.

"We've found you a husband," he said.

He opened his wallet and took out a passport photograph. The man in the small black-and-white picture looked nice enough, though perhaps not as handsome as Rahel might have hoped.

"His name is Fadhil," said her mother. "His English is very good."

"He looks pretty serious," said Rahel.

Her father shrugged. "It is just a photograph."

"Will I get a chance to speak to him?"

"Next month," said her father. "He is coming here."

"What? To stay?"

"He has already bought the ticket," her mother nodded.

Rahel wondered if the ticket was one way or return.

Brian looked surprised when Rahel told him the news.

"Aren't you too young to be tying the knot?"

"I'm seventeen. That's how old my mom was."

"You gonna check this guy out when he gets here?"

"I guess so."

"Does he know what he's getting himself into?"

"Stop teasing me."

"Don't get me wrong," said Brian, "but in my day you'd meet the girl first—at a dance, maybe—then you'd ask for her parents' permission."

"It doesn't sound so different," said Rahel.

"Except that you got to dance with her first," said Brian.

Fadhil arrived with his mother. Rahel was at the airport with her family to meet them. She stood behind the barrier and watched the endless line of people filing past. There were businessmen in expensive suits, and curly-haired boys her own age who smiled mischievously at her. Fadhil was almost the last to come out. His clothes were old-fashioned and rumpled from the long flight. When he looked at Rahel, he didn't smile.

Fadhil introduced himself and his mother. He nodded at Rahel, but spoke to her brothers. His mother took Rahel's hand and kissed her lightly on the cheek.

"You did not need to come to the airport," she said, in the old language. "You should have stayed at home."

Back at the house, they celebrated with a big meal. Then afterward, Rahel cleared the table while her parents discussed the wedding plans with Fadhil and his mother.

"She must choose her own dress, of course," said the

old woman, "but please make it something traditional. I am not used to these modern fashions."

It was decided that after the wedding the couple would continue to live with Rahel's family until her husband had enough money to support her. It wasn't clear whether Fadhil's mother would stay on or return to the old country, though Rahel heard her say she wasn't ready for such a big change.

"So what's this guy like?" asked Brian.

"Hard to know," said Rahel. "He doesn't say much."

"Still waters run deep, 'eh?"

"It's over my head," said Rahel.

Rahel had no sisters, so Fadhil and his mother were given her bedroom and Rahel had to sleep on the couch. In the days that followed, Rahel worked hard to make a good impression. She was charming and considerate. She cooked the meals and cleaned the house. She mended clothes and dug in the garden. But Fadhil was often out at the café, playing cards with her father.

It was almost a week before he asked about her job at the supermarket.

"I work in the meat section," she told him.

Fadhil looked at his mother. "Has it been blessed?" he asked.

Rahel shook her head.

Fadhil frowned. "But our religion forbids it."

Rahel looked at her father, who looked away. "It's no big deal," she said.

Fadhil's mother shook her head.

"You are forbidden," said Fadhil. "As your husband, I forbid you."

"You're not my husband yet," said Rahel.

"It is not right," said Fadhil. "Do you understand?"

"Totally," Rahel murmured. "There's no need to freak."

"Excuse me?"

"I'm getting the picture," said Rahel.

When Rahel tried explaining it to Brian, he couldn't see the problem.

"If you don't want to touch the meat," he said, "just wear rubber gloves."

"But I promised Fadhil," she said.

"I won't tell him if you don't."

"But he'll go berserk."

"Not if he doesn't find out, he won't."

The butchers worked at the back of the supermarket in a long, brightly lit room behind a door that said *Staff Only*. There was a window looking out into the store, but Brian told Rahel she could work out of sight at the other end if she wanted to.

So Rahel continued to work in the meat section. There were rump steaks, lamb chops, pork sausages, chopped meat, and chicken fillets. Rahel weighed each tray of meat, wrapped it in plastic, and stuck on the price. When the butchers had gone home, she hosed down the floors, wiped the benches, and cleaned the knives. She wore an apron and carried a change of clothes, just in case. She washed her hands repeatedly throughout the day. To prepare Halal meat, according to traditional law, the animal's head must be turned to face Mecca and a prayer said as it is slaughtered. Sometimes Rahel found herself saying a prayer for all the unblessed animals whose carcasses had ended up there. Sometimes she even said a prayer for the pigs. And whenever Fadhil asked about her work, Rahel told him a different story. She was sweeping floors and stacking shelves, she said. She was making coffee and taking phone messages. She was running errands and helping customers.

"You must be a very good worker," said Fadhil, with a strange smile.

It didn't feel good, lying to him like that.

Things did not improve between Rahel and her future mother-in-law. Fadhil's mother didn't believe it was right for a guest to do housework, but she followed Rahel around, making comments about how things were done differently in the old country. She was charming with Rahel's parents, but silent when Rahel spoke. Rahel felt the disapproval in her gaze.

With her son, Fadhil's mother was entirely different. She would comb his hair and straighten his collar. She made his bed and insisted on washing his clothes by hand. At the dinner table she would offer him food from her own plate and constantly fuss over him like a child. Fadhil would just smile and say, "Really, Mother, you should not worry."

Most mornings, Fadhil went out with the other men. He would come home for the evening meal, then sit on the couch watching TV. As the weeks went by, Fadhil spoke to Rahel less and less. If his mother was in the room, he seemed uncomfortable even to be sharing a couch with his future wife.

Rahel wondered how much money he was spending and where he was getting it from. She dreaded to think how things would be, once they were married and living in their own house.

When she tried talking to her father about it, he wouldn't listen.

"Fadhil will make a good husband," he said.

"You don't know anything about him," said Rahel.

"He comes from a good family. He respects his mother."

"Is that all you care about? Don't you want me to be happy?"

"You want love and romance, like you see on TV. But when you are married, you will understand these things better."

"When I am married, it will be too late."

* * *

At the supermarket, the boys unloaded meat from the truck, hung the carcasses on rail hooks, and shunted them off to the freezer, one by one. When Rahel had finished cleaning the meat room, she dragged the remaining hooks back to the freezer and closed the big metal door. She undid her apron and threw it in the laundry bin. She washed her hands in the sink and checked that her clothes were clean. She thought about her father and mother, and whether theirs was an equal marriage. She thought about having her own children one day, and what kind of father Fadhil would be. She thought about the traditions of the old country and how much they had changed in just one generation. How could she be expected to keep the old traditions when so much had already changed?

In the delivery bay, hanging from the weight scales, there was one last meat hook she must have overlooked. Making sure that no one was watching, Rahel jumped up and grabbed hold of the hook, as she had seen the boys do when they were clowning around. She hung from the meat hook, trying to measure her own weight, then dropped to the floor when she heard footsteps coming along the corridor.

"Hangin' around after work, eh?"

It was Brian.

Rahel stood there, her cheeks burning with embarrassment.

"There's a guy here to see you," said Brian. "He looks pretty agitated."

Fadhil was waiting at the register. He smiled when he saw her, but his smile quickly disappeared. They nodded, but didn't touch. When she looked at her hands, she noticed a speck of meat had wedged itself under one fingernail. It must have happened while she was hanging from the hook. Rahel was sure from the way Fadhil was frowning that he had come to check up on her. If he noticed the meat, then she was in trouble.

"You came to see me?"

"I look for you, but you are busy."

"I just finished."

Fadhil stared at her intensely. "I am to be your husband," he said, as if beginning a well-rehearsed speech. "If you are to be my wife, it is important that you respect me."

When Rahel looked into his dark, piercing eyes, she felt afraid. He was from another country. His culture was not the same as hers. But why should *she* change? This was *her* country. It was *her* culture.

"It's important to respect each *other*," she said, feeling her courage return.

"If you are to respect me," Fadhil continued, "I must prove myself worthy of respect."

He looked slightly crazy, she thought.

"When I look before, I see you through the window. I see you clean the knives. I have such a strong feeling. I want to go in there, but the manager he stop me."

"Did you come here to spy on me?"

"I come to see you. I cannot wait any longer."

"If you have something to tell me, then say it."

Fadhil took a deep breath. "I get the job!" he said proudly.

"You've got a job?"

"As a cutter in the slaughterhouse. It is not Halal, but it is very good job. I start tomorrow!" Fadhil took her hand and held it gently. "I am a lucky man. I am given a beautiful wife. Now I can work to support her."

"What about our religion? Don't you care about unclean animals?"

"Of course. They are forbidden."

"What about the pigs?"

Fadhil frowned. "I try some bacon once. It taste very greasy."

Rahel laughed. "You're supposed to cook it first."

Fadhil grinned at her. "Do not tell my mother," he said. "I am sure she will be totally freaked."

ACCOUNTS

Louisa was awakened in the night by a loud knock on the front door.

"Whoever it is," her mother called out, "tell them to go away."

Louisa put on her robe and went to see who it was. The man at the door was older than her mother. One side of his shirt was untucked, and his breath smelled strongly of alcohol.

"Jackie there?" he mumbled, trying to push past her.

Louisa blocked his way. "She's in bed. You can't come in."

"Who's she got in there? Another happy customer?"

"She wants you to go away."

"I don't care what she wants."

Louisa stood her ground. "I need to sleep. No one's here and it's going to stay that way. I have an exam in the morning."

The man hesitated. "She owes me fifty bucks."

"Wait here," said Louisa.

She closed the door and got the money from her wallet, then she gave it to the stranger and said good night. When she went back inside the house, her mother was sitting on the couch. Louisa noticed a reddish-brown smudge around her mouth. On the coffee table was an empty bottle of iron tablets.

"How many of those did you have?"

Her mother looked away. "Five or six. I don't know."

"Mom! That jar was full."

Louisa called a taxi and took her mother to the hospital. The two of them sat in a tiny cubicle, waiting to be seen. Louisa tried not to think about her Anatomy exam in the morning. Finally, a doctor examined Jackie and sent her up for an X-ray.

The radiology room was cold and gray, and the equipment looked terribly out-of-date. Jackie was upset and could not lie still long enough for the X-ray machine to work. Louisa had to put on a protective gown and come out from behind the safety screen to hold her mother's hand.

"I don't want to die," Jackie whimpered. "I was just trying to cheer myself up."

"It's okay, Mom. We'll be out of here soon."

"You should have told me they were dangerous."

"I know, Mom. I'm sorry."

AI$LE

Bending down into the freezer, Stephen removed the packages of frozen peas and stacked them, one by one, on top of the frozen beans. At the bottom, underneath the metal grille, was a CD case with his name on it. Keeping his compact discs at low temperatures improved their performance and gave them a longer life. The bottom of the freezer was also an ideal hiding place.

Stephen brushed the ice off the CD case. He unzipped a backpack containing his Gameboy, towel, toothbrush, and a change of clothes. He hid the CDs in a secret compartment where no one would think to look. Without saying goodbye to the people he had worked with for almost two years, Stephen slipped away unnoticed through the front door of the supermarket. He caught a bus into the city and was never heard from again.

* * *

Stephen loved his computer even more than he loved his mother. And Stephen loved his mother very much, because ever since he was six years old she had let him have unlimited time on his computer. Late into the night he would sit there in his bedroom, building and destroying entire civilizations, massacring barbarians and innocent tribes alike. Stephen was a mighty warrior and a powerful foe. He wanted to rule mankind with an iron fist, to control the greatest armies in the land and rewrite history as the world's most powerful emperor. But every time Stephen came close to winning, victory would slip through his fingers. His supply lines would be cut off and his armies would run out of food. His golden palaces would be destroyed and his empire would go bankrupt. His weapons of war would become outdated and the enemy would rise up against him. Stephen would fight to the bitter end, but the enemy were too numerous, too skilled, or too technologically sophisticated, and they always won.

It really annoyed him.

Stephen lived with his mother most of the time, but when things weren't working out, he went to stay with his father. Both Stephen's parents had important government jobs. They worked long hours and didn't come home until late at night. It didn't bother Stephen, though. He had keys to both their houses and so did his sister, Penny. Stephen and his older sister rarely spoke to each other. They had gone to different schools and had always led parallel lives. When their parents had separated, Penny told Stephen it was normal. Lots of kids had parents who were divorced, she said, and mostly the ones who stayed married didn't love each other anyway. Love was something that happened in the movies, Penny said, not in real life.

Most days, Stephen's mother would leave him alone, but every once in a while, she would insist on having some quality time. Quality time meant going out for dinner together and his mother asking him questions like, "What did you do today?" "How's the job going?" "Have you ever thought of studying more?" But if Stephen tried to talk about his latest battle, his mother's smile would freeze and her head would start to nod up and down. He would ask about her day, so he didn't have to talk. She would tell him about press releases, guidelines, deadlines, draft papers, budget meetings, and memos for the governor. She would say, "I'm boring you, aren't I?" but then keep on talking. Until finally, she would say, "I *am* boring you. I know it." She would give him a kiss, then they would go home.

Stephen hated being kissed by his mother.

At the supermarket, Stephen rarely spoke. While the staff were taking their break, he sat in a corner playing on his Gameboy. If anyone ever asked him a question, he'd give them the shortest answer he could think of.

"Hey, Stephen. How's it going?"

"Good."

Stephen worked twelve hours a week in Frozen Foods, unloading the refrigerated delivery trucks and stacking the freezers single-handedly. Carting boxes at subzero temperatures was not the kind of job that workers put their hands up for, but Stephen didn't mind. It kept people away from him, and that was how he liked it. At home, he was paid pocket money to make his bed and put his dirty clothes in the wash. Most days, he forgot to do both, but his mother paid him anyway. She was too busy to bother arguing.

When he wasn't working, which was most of the time, Stephen was on the Internet, under the pseudonym of *GHOSTYX*: "ghost" plus "Styx"—the river of dead souls. He joined forces with *PROTON SLUG* and *CHAOS OVERLORD*, and together the three great warriors would slaughter legions and turn entire cities to dust. It was a good feeling, going into battle with friends by your side. It was a good feeling, having friends you'd never met. Stephen's body was in his room, but his brain had logged on to an invisible world. He locked his door and put on headphones. If his sister came home, or his mother knocked, he would pretend not to hear them. He was lost with his cyber-friends inside a virtual labyrinth, fighting imaginary demons, surviving from one battle to the next. They were just women, doing whatever it was that women did.

Then, one fateful day, Stephen received an important e-mail.

Do you desire to meet the ICE MAIDEN?

Stephen knew about the dangers of downloading viruses, but he was intrigued.

He clicked on [Yes].

Are you pure of heart?

Stephen wasn't, but he clicked on [Yes] anyway.

Do you wish to be skilled in the ways of elemental magic?

Stephen clicked on [Yes] and waited for the program to download.

Five hundred years ago in South America, it said, *a teenage Incan girl was sacrificed to the gods. She was taken by the priests high up into the mountains and left there to freeze to death. There was a storm that night and the mountain was covered in snow. The girl was buried alive and frozen in the ice. Centuries later, her body was discovered. She became known as the Ice Maiden.*

Stephen looked at the picture of the girl's mummified face and body. It sent a shiver down his spine.

He clicked on [More].

But the Ice Maiden was not what she appeared to be. By unearthing her body, the men had unleashed the wrath of the gods. The Ice Maiden became a powerful enchantress, a cruel spirit who had come to torment mankind with mortal desire. Whenever men looked upon her, the Ice Maiden would ensnare them. With her perfect beauty, her mysterious arts and

allurements, she would entice them into a shadow world, from
which there was no escape.

Stephen looked at the picture of the Ice Maiden with her perfect, untouchable breasts. There was no doubt about it. She was totally hot.

Do you wish to know more?

Stephen clicked on [Yes].

Do you worship my perfect beauty?

[Yes].

Do you desire no other but me?

[Yes].

Do you surrender yourself completely?

[Yes].

Stephen's life began to change. With the help of the Ice Maiden, he discovered new powers. She could turn his medieval warriors into lethal cyborgs who walked across water to destroy the pitiful enemy, hand-to-hand. Instead of spears and arrows, they fired laser beams and particle rays. Instead of burning oil, his catapults shot nuclear warheads. With the enchantress by his side, Stephen was invincible. He was more than a great emperor now. He was a god.

Stephen's two-dimensional game-world had become more real than the three-dimensional world. (Or had the real world become unimaginably one-dimensional?) At work, he found it harder and harder to concentrate.

Nothing seemed worth doing any more. It was all point-
less, hopeless, useless. He felt trapped, condemned to
spend the rest of his life in a freezer. He found himself
staring at girls and the way their hips moved as they carried their shopping baskets or pushed their carts. There
were good girls like Louisa and bad girls like Chloe. The
good girls were perfect and the bad girls were dangerous.
But when Louisa asked him to give her a hand with some
boxes, what was that all about? And when Chloe called
him a sleaze, was that just a part of the game?

Stephen didn't know anything about girls, but with the
Ice Maiden beside him, he didn't need to.

He had noticed a change in his sister. Almost overnight, it
seemed, Penny had turned into a hippie. There were pots
of lentil stew on the stove, and garlic on the kitchen table.
He noticed the smell of incense wafting through the
house and in the laundry room he found a moon chart
and planting calendar. Now, when they passed in the hall,
Penny smiled at him in that sad, hippie way. Her clothes
were more colorful and she was always going out, to do
whatever it was that hippies did. It really annoyed him.

While Penny was in the house, Stephen stayed in his
room. He waited until she went to her room before he
came out to eat. But it was the stuff she left lying around
that really bothered him. Everything Penny owned was
either hand-made or organically grown. It was as if the

twentieth century had never happened. And even when he found nothing, Stephen felt a kind of disturbance, just knowing Penny was in the house. Why couldn't she move out? Wasn't there a commune or farming collective that would have her?

Stephen was tired of sharing his house with a hippie. In fact, he was tired of sharing altogether. In his quest to appease the enchantress, he betrayed his Internet friends. After luring their armies into the Valley of the Shadow, he decimated *PROTON SLUG* and obliterated *CHAOS OVERLORD*. Finally, he was the supreme ruler!

But victory brought little glory for *GHOSTYX*. Like the taste of old chewing gum, it was flat and flavorless, something to be spit out or rolled up and stuck somewhere out of sight. After hours of sitting at the computer, with the bedroom door shut and curtains closed, his skin felt cold and his legs had begun to go numb. He could almost feel the ice dripping from the ceiling, like stalactites.

Stephen got up to go to the bathroom. It was a sunny day outside. The sky was blue and the birds were singing. He rubbed his eyes as he looked out the window. In the backyard, Penny was digging in the vegetable garden. Stephen could hardly believe what he saw. He looked away, then he looked back again, just to be sure. His sister had on a hippie skirt that went down to her muddy boots, but that was it. From the waist up she was wearing nothing. Her breasts were tanned. She was topless!

Stephen felt like he was going to be sick. He tried going to the bathroom, but couldn't. He hurried back to his bedroom and locked the door behind him. He sat at his computer, trying not to think about what he had just seen, trying to abort the major download that was going on inside his head. Instead of reopening his current file, Stephen typed in his secret password and accessed the hard drive. As he scrolled through the countless Ice Maiden sites he had visited over the past months, he thought of his mother and what she would say if she found them.

Do you wish to erase entire history?

Stephen clicked on [Yes].

Are you sure?

[Yes]

Stephen clicked on [Exit] then he pushed [Control] + [Escape] just to be certain.

Stephen took the frozen packages from the freezer and stacked them up, one by one. He removed his CD case from its hiding place at the bottom, brushed off the ice, and hid it in his backpack. Invisible as a cold draft, Stephen left the supermarket and caught a bus into the city. From there, he called his mother and left a message on her machine.

"I've gone to stay at Dad's."

His mother waited two weeks before finally calling her ex-husband to find out what was happening. She left a message on his machine, then he left a message on hers. By the time they actually spoke to each other, Stephen was living in another city. He was working in a morgue, part-time. He had a new computer and a new e-mail account under a different name. Only his pseudonym remained.

DELIVERY BAY

Adam arrived at work to find the supermarket in half darkness. There had been a power failure in the night. The emergency lights were on at the front entrance and the registers were still working. Customers continued pushing carts and comparing prices as if nothing had happened, even though the rest of the store was in twilight.

Out the back, the storeroom was in chaos. There was no emergency lighting. The air-conditioning had gone off. A sickly-sweet smell of rotting fruit, fermented vegetables, and rancid butter filled the air. There were screams and flashing torches. Workers were scaring each other with spooky noises and glowing ghost faces. They were tearing open boxes and throwing food around. It wasn't like a supermarket anymore. It was a jungle.

Pure anarchy, thought Adam. It was like a dream come true.

Until he saw Louisa.

She was there in the delivery bay with some of the night staff who had stayed on after their shift. The three boys were chasing a rat. It was huge and slow—either half dead from rat poison or else dying of high cholesterol. As it tried to escape, one of them caught its tail, but the rat wriggled free. Adam watched it shuffle off toward Louisa and disappear into the boxes. He noticed how Louisa was not afraid of the rat. She was also not afraid of the night boys.

"Leave it alone," she told them. And they did.

Adam saw it happen and he understood: This wasn't pure anarchy anymore. It was the opposite. Finally, he knew what he had to do.

Plan A was awful. Plan B was bad. Plan C was crucial. What was the best way to impress an Employee of the Month? Adam decided, then and there, to become the perfect worker. He would be punctual and well-dressed. His shoes would be polished, his clothes would be ironed. He would always wear clean, matching socks. He would improve his personal hygiene. He would cut his finger-nails. He would shave every morning and put on after-shave. He would comb his hair, clean his teeth, and floss daily. He would hold his head up and look people in the eye. He would stop saying "Yeah," "Nah," "Um," and "What?" He would never swear or pick his nose. He would show initiative. He would give 100 percent. He

would be a team player. He would be honest, but respect-
ful. He would listen to instructions, follow procedures,
keep to deadlines. He would never make excuses, never
complain. He would be aware of safety issues. He would
learn where all the stock was kept. He would be polite to
customers and listen to their complaints. He would get
along with his coworkers and be kind to rats. Everyone
would be very impressed, especially Louisa. Until, finally,
when he was least expecting it, she would tell him how
impressed she was, and he would casually reply, "Do you
know who my inspiration is?"

The rest, he imagined, would be history.

From out of the gloom at the far end of the storeroom,
the door to the meat room opened and a dim light appeared. At first Adam could not make it out, as the glowing shape moved slowly toward him.

Someone screamed.

"What *is* that?" said Louisa.

Mounted on a stake, tied to a shopping cart pushed by
Jared and Dylan, was a pig's head with a flashlight in its
mouth. The flashlight illuminated the animal's pink flesh
and shone from its snout, giving it a laughing smile. Its
eyes were hollow shadows and its skin was eerily human.
It almost looked alive.

"Behold! And fear for your souls!"

"The Lord of the Shelves has returned!"

AISLE 10

Wyn was in aisle 10, checking the stock. She waved "the Max" across the item barcode and the hand-held computer gizmo displayed the name "Thick 'n Chunky Hot Pot," its price, weight, and the amount of stock remaining. Wyn's fingers flashed across the keys as she entered the four-digit item code and reordered new stock from the warehouse, to be delivered the following day.

When she looked up, a lady customer was watching her.

"I was looking for Japanese miso soup," she said. "They told me to ask you. They said you'd know where it was."

Wyn nodded and the woman followed her along the aisle.

"We sell the paste," she said, taking a package from the shelf and giving it to her.

The woman read the label. "Are you sure this is it?"

"Just add boiling water," said Wyn.

"That's all?"

"Then spring onions, tofu, mushrooms, whatever you like."

"Are you Japanese?" the woman asked.

"No," said Wyn.

"Then how do you know?"

"I read the package."

"Do you read all the packages?" the woman asked.

"Yes," said Wyn.

No one in the store knew as much as Wyn. Her coworkers called her "the Max" because, like the gizmo, she had an encyclopedic knowledge of the items on the shelves. Wyn knew where everything was and what it was used for. She knew the difference between pickles and chutneys, fine-grade and choice-grade meat, arabica and robusta coffee beans, barn-laid and free-range eggs. She knew what toilet paper was bleach-free, which sausages were gluten-free, which tuna was dolphin-friendly, and what tomato juice contained no added salt. Wyn knew which birdseed contained shell grit, which shampoo contained henna, which dim sums had no MSG, and which tea had no tannic acid. She knew what percentage of which drinks was real fruit juice and what amount of eucalyptus oil could kill you. She knew where the avocadoes had come from and whether they were ripe yet.

It wasn't just the shelves that she knew about. Wyn had an almost miraculous ability to see into the lives of other people. Alcoholics, chocoholics, workaholics, shopaholics. Wyn was not psychic, but by taking note of what people bought, she was able to deduce the most intimate and personal facts about them.

"Happy anniversary! I hope your husband remembers this year!"

"You're looking much better since you gave up smoking."

"That new hair color suits you, I think."

"How is Rex? Has he stopped chewing the furniture yet?"

Wyn was friendly with everyone, and everyone was friendly with Wyn. Her conversations were always light and chatty, but with her Sherlock Holmes–like powers of observation, Wyn was able to know more about a person than they might have wished. She knew that Graham's "business lunches" were actually golf games with his friends; that Amanda was having an affair with Shane, the racist storeroom manager; that Gavin, the night manager, had irritable bowel syndrome; and that Brian, the meat manager, took pills for high cholesterol. She knew that Cameron, the produce manager, and Scott, the trainee manager, had slept with Chloe on the same night and that Nicola, the dairy manager, had been so upset she had taken a week off to get over it. Wyn knew that Rahel went to the movies even though she was not allowed. She knew that Jared was selling drugs, Dylan was seeing a therapist, Emma had ratted on Tessa, and Abdi was wasting his money on scratch-off lottery tickets. She knew about Adam and Louisa.

But Wyn was not a gossip. What she knew, she never spoke of.

In the supermarket, when a register was full, the money was counted and put in a plastic bag. The bag was sealed and placed in a chute, where it got sucked up a pipe along the ceiling to the accounts office. The accounts office was a small room with a service window and a locked door. The woman who worked there counted the money and prepared the pay slips. Her name was Bev, and every day she wore new clothes, even though she only ever left the office to get a sandwich.

Wyn knocked on the accounts office door and Bev unlocked it.

"Quyen?"

"It's pronounced 'Wyn,' " said Wyn, politely.

"I'm sorry, sweetie," said Bev.

"You asked to see me?" said Wyn.

Bev offered her a chair. "Please," she said. "Sit down."

Wyn sat down on the edge of her chair.

"Would you like a cup of coffee, sweetie?"

"No."

"A glass of water?"

"No."

"So," Bev smiled warmly. "You're finishing school soon?"

"Yes."

"Were you planning on going to university?"

"I want to be a librarian," said Wyn.

Bev nodded thoughtfully. "Are you happy here, sweetie?"

"Yes."

"I imagine you can guess why I wanted to see you?"

"To offer me a job?"

"Not just a job," said Bev. "There's a vacancy for a full-time, permanent position! I wondered if you were interested?"

Wyn smiled politely. "Is it to work in this office?"

"Initially," Bev nodded. "But, as you know, in a big company like this, there are excellent opportunities."

The phone rang and Bev picked it up. Her voice changed as she said the name of the company, the store location, her own name and *How may I help you?* in a single flawless sentence. Bev listened briefly, then with the same perfect delivery, she advised the caller that the store was open twenty-four hours, seven days a week. Then she thanked the caller for phoning and hung up.

"I've checked with management," she said, as if the phone call had never happened. "The job's yours, sweetie, if you want it."

"But I haven't found out about my college applications yet."

"You could always defer."

"I like books," said Wyn quietly.

"I *love* books," said Bev. "But the question is, where do you see yourself being, ten years from now?"

"I need time to think about it," said Wyn.

Bev got up and unlocked the door for her.

"Of course," she said. "Think it over and let me know."

For Chinese New Year, Wyn's family celebrated with a special feast. There were spring rolls and honey prawns, seaweed and whole baked fish, bean pies and stir-fried noodles, sticky rice and moon cakes. Everyone in Wyn's family was there. At the head of the table, her grandmother sat on two cushions, giving the children red envelopes containing money.

"What is the matter, Wyn?" the old woman asked. "You are gloomy."

Wyn tried to smile. She knew it was important to be happy, in order to be happy for the rest of the new year.

"Wyn was offered a promotion," said her mother. "She has to decide between working in a library and working in a shop."

"It's a supermarket chain," said her father.

"It's still a shop," said her mother.

"What's the money like?" asked her uncle.

"She's not sure," said her mother.

"How can you make a decision, before you know the starting salary?" said her uncle. "Are you crazy?"

"This fish is delicious," said her aunt. "I must get the recipe."

"If she does the librarian course," said her father, "it will be another year before she even has an income."

"Three years, if she does the degree course," said her mother.

"And there's no guarantee she will find a job at the end of it," said her father.

"Aren't libraries downsizing because of the Internet?" said her brother.

"It won't be long before everyone is reading e-books," said her cousin.

"An e-book is still a book," said her mother.

"In terms of opportunities," said her brother. "I know which one I'd be choosing."

"Likewise," said her cousin.

"What about overtime and holidays?" asked her uncle.

"She's not sure," said her mother.

"Are you crazy?" said her uncle. "Don't they have a union?"

"Who cares about unions?" said her father. "What did unions ever do for anyone?"

"The noodles are good," said her aunt. "But too spicy for me."

"Not for me," said her brother.

"Likewise," said her cousin.

"Wyn has always loved books," said her mother.

"Being a librarian doesn't mean sitting around reading all day," said her father.

"In some ways," said her aunt, "a supermarket is like a library, with food on the shelves instead of books."

"Maybe Wyn should work in a bookshop," said her brother.

"Selling cookbooks!" said her cousin.

"What about a pension?" said her uncle.

"What about health benefits?" said her father.

"In a library?" said her uncle. "Are you crazy?"

"Anyone who works in a library is sure to end up needing glasses," said her father.

"What happens if a bookshelf falls on her?" said her cousin.

"Even libraries have workers' comp and liability insurance," said her brother.

"What about the bean pies?" said her aunt. "Has anyone tried the bean pies?"

"As far as I'm concerned," said her father, "there's no such thing as the perfect job. You work for the money, and the harder you work, the sooner you can retire."

"Wyn could do whatever she put her mind to," said her mother. "Her teacher suggested she study psychology."

"What's psychology?" asked her little sister.

"It's for people who are crazy," said her uncle.

"Eat up, everyone," said her aunt. "There's so much food left!"

"Do you really want our daughter to spend the rest of her life listening to crazy people?" said her father.

Wyn looked at her grandmother, but neither of them spoke.

"She doesn't want to study psychology," said her little sister. "She wants to be a librarian."

After the meal, a plate of fortune cookies was passed around and people read out their lucky messages:

Different flowers look good to different people, said one.

Once you pour water out of a bucket, it's hard to get it back in, said another.

Even the most clever housewife cannot cook without rice, said a third.

Wyn sat and listened, but none of it seemed very helpful.

On the stroke of midnight they opened all the windows to let the old year go away. Outside, in the garden, Wyn's brother set off firecrackers to scare away bad luck, then her uncle began launching the fireworks. Wyn and her grandmother stood on the grass, watching as each rocket shot up into the sky and exploded with bright colors. It was a new year. A new beginning.

Wyn took the old lady's hand and squeezed it tight.

"What should I do, Grandmother?"

The old woman shook her head.

"It isn't up to me to decide," she said. "You must ask yourself, *What do I want?*"

"I want my family to be proud of me," said Wyn. "I want to be successful."

"Do you want to be happy?" asked her grandmother.

"Of course," said Wyn.

"If you are happy," she said, "then you are successful."

"Did you like working in the clothes factory, Grandmother?"

"Yes. Do you like working in the supermarket?"

"Yes, but I also like books."

"Working in a supermarket is a good job to have."

"I know, Grandmother."

Together, they watched the last bottle rocket fall back to earth in a fountain of light.

The old woman smiled.

"It's a good job to have," she said, "while you study to be a librarian."

ACCOUNTS

Bev the accountant was talking on the phone. Louisa watched through the little window of her office, waiting for her to hang up. She looked at Bev's desk, with the neatly labeled folders, the sharpened pencils, the coffee cup with her name on it, and the framed photos of her two beautiful children. There was a fern in the corner and a picture on the wall. Bev had worked hard to make it feel like home.

When the phone call was finished, Louisa knocked softly on the door and Bev opened it.

"Come in, sweetie," she said. "I bet you can guess why I wanted to see you?"

It was seven o'clock by the time Louisa got home from work. Her mother was in the kitchen eating her microwaved dinner from its plastic container. Louisa said hello, but Jackie didn't answer. On the table in front of her there were several bills with *OVERDUE* stamped across them in big red letters.

"Why haven't you paid them?" Louisa asked.

Jackie shook her head. "We've got no money."

Louisa told herself to stay calm. "What about my account?"

Jackie frowned at her like a resentful three-year-old.

"I borrowed it, okay? I'll pay you back."

"You mean you've gambled it all away? I should never have given you my PIN."

Three-year-old resentment turned to three-year-old self-pity. Jackie pushed her dinner away. "What I do is my own business!"

Louisa's face flushed with anger. "Not when you're throwing away my money!"

"Don't worry, I'll pay you back."

"When?"

"When I get the money, of course."

"When you win it, you mean?"

"What I do is my own business," Jackie repeated.

This was the way it always went. The conversation became a snake chasing its own tail. It spun and spun until it ended up eating itself.

But this time Louisa wasn't having it.

"I've covered for you long enough, Mom! I'm not doing it anymore," she snapped. "It isn't just your business. It's my business, too. The more I do for you, the more you expect me to do. I'm not supposed to be looking after you. I'm the child! You're supposed to be the mother!"

AISLE 11

Marco, the night security guard, was waiting for the 2:00 a.m. freak show. Every night it was the same. You could set your watch by it. The freaks arrived, disheveled and bleary-eyed, in their dirty jeans, their secondhand clothes, even their *pajamas*, would you believe? They were like another species, blinded by the fluorescent lights and feeling their way around the store in search of the ultimate munchie food. But it wasn't chocolate they were interested in. It wasn't the snack foods or even the cookies. Night after night, like turtles drawn by instinct toward the same moonlit beach, the freaks arrived mysteriously at 2:00 a.m. and dragged themselves along aisle 11. They bought cupcakes and fruit muffins and loaves of soft white bread, jars of peanut butter and strawberry jam, easy-squeeze bottles of honey and cream-cheese spread. Elvis food, Marco called it. And the freaks could not get enough of it.

Not that Marco had anything against Elvis. Far from it. With his sulky good looks, his jet-black hair, and long sideburns, Marco even looked like the King, some said. Not that he needed to advertise it. He wasn't about to embarrass himself in an Elvis look-alike competition. Imagine putting on a rhinestone jumpsuit and making a fool of yourself, only to be told at the end of it that someone else looked *more* like the King than you did. After all, there was only one *real* Elvis Presley. Marco didn't know if Elvis had left the building or not. He'd read the stories. He knew the jury was still out on that one. If the 2:00 a.m. freaks wanted to deep-fry their peanut-butter sandwiches, he wasn't going to stop them. But it *was* a tragedy, all the same. How could someone as talented as Elvis, so good-looking and so rich, become such a big fat loser?

As he paced the floor of the supermarket, Marco's shoes made tiny squeaking sounds on the linoleum floor. He passed the contract cleaners with their gray overalls and grim faces. He nodded at the stock clerks, tearing open their cardboard boxes. He smiled at the girl behind the register. Every night, Marco walked the same circuit around the perimeter of the store. He did it in the same number of footsteps, give or take, with the same number of squeaks. Five times an hour, eight hours a night, his feet fell in the same places, avoided the same cracks, and cut the same corners. But that was the job.

Marco liked to think about Elvis. The King had the Colonel to organize his business affairs. He had a wife and a beautiful daughter. He had legions of adoring fans and the Memphis Mafia to protect him. He had women falling at his feet. But what the King had really needed, more than anything, was a personal trainer. If Marco had been Elvis's personal trainer, he would have known what to do. First, he would have started with some cardio-vascular work, some weight training, and some gentle stretches. A stroll around Graceland for a bit of fresh air. And a stricter diet, of course. The chocolate banana sundaes would have had to go. It would have been a challenge, especially at the end there, when Elvis could hardly get up out of his chair. But with a bit of willpower and positive thinking, who knows? When the King was in better shape physically, then one could tackle the more complicated business of rebuilding his self-esteem and confidence. In life, Marco believed, there were winners and losers. With the right motivation, provided by a top-notch personal trainer and life coach, the King might have taken control of his destiny and realized his enormous potential. By setting the right goals and harnessing the raw power of the mind, Elvis might have gone back on the road and into the studio. Who knows? History might have been rewritten.

"Black Knight to the front desk . . . Could Black Knight please come to the front desk?"

The announcement snapped Marco out of his reverie. He stopped walking and for a split second his foot seemed to hover uncertainly in the air. Something was up, something important. The King would just have to wait.

Gavin the night manager was at the front desk, looking hassled. Marco followed him out of the store and through the empty food court. At the doors to the shopping center, Gavin stopped and pointed across the empty parking lot.

"See those kids," he said. "They're off their faces. Go and tell them to leave, before they do something stupid."

There were five kids, each carrying a plastic bag with the supermarket logo on it. They were passing around an aerosol spray can. One after another, they filled their plastic bags and inhaled the fumes. They were fourteen years old, maybe, and looking for trouble. As Marco watched, one of them picked up a bottle and smashed it against a wall.

"Do you think we should call the police?" he asked.

"I don't want you to arrest them," said Gavin. "Just tell them to go away."

Marco didn't think much of Gavin. His clothes were shabby, his hair was a mess, and he never did much managing, as far as Marco could see. While the big trucks were making their deliveries and the shopping cart boys were whizzing around the aisles like an all-night Grand Prix, Gavin stayed in his office, painting his toenails, most likely. Maybe that was the skill of a good manager. Maybe the man was more organized than Marco gave him credit for. But Marco was sure of one thing. He wasn't taking a bullet for Gavin.

"They look pretty wired," said Marco uncertainly.

Gavin took out a walkie-talkie like the one on Marco's belt.

"Stay in touch," he said. "And don't take any crap."

Marco walked out into the parking lot feeling very conspicuous. His shoes were squeaking loudly and he probably should have gone to the bathroom first. *Remember the power of positive thinking*, he told himself. He tried to show it in the way he walked and in the look on his face. It was essential to maintain self-esteem. He was a winner and they were losers. It was as simple as that.

Halfway across the parking lot, before the gang had even noticed him, Marco stopped and called out to them in a loud, authoritative voice, "Clear out, you guys!"

The kids in the gang turned around and looked at him. Marco stood still, with his hands by his sides. Not like a gunslinger, exactly. More like the King in *Viva Las Vegas*, standing in the spotlight, all eyes on his every move.

"You heard me!"

There was a moment of uncertainty. A flicker of doubt seemed to pass through the gang. Then they laughed at him.

Marco reached for his walkie-talkie, so they would see he wasn't alone.

"What's happening?" asked Gavin. "Everything under control?"

"No drama," Marco reported.

When Marco turned around, the night manager was standing there behind the glass door, looking like an idiot. How could a person in Marco's position possibly establish his authority while this jerk was watching his every move?

"Do you think we should send for backup?" he asked.

"What do you need?" said Gavin. "A tank division?"

Marco didn't need a tank division, but he wished he had a gun. Not to shoot them with, of course. Just to scare them. The gun wouldn't even need to be loaded. In fact, a water pistol would do the job. Marco wished he had something more than just a two-way radio. Even a big stick would have been handy. He weighed his options. Obviously he would have to move closer. With his powers of positive thinking, combined with his greater experience and commanding yet relaxed presence, these young losers would soon know who they were dealing with.

As Marco walked up to them, the gang spread out into a line. They were mean-looking kids, there was no doubt about it. They were older and taller than they looked from a distance. And they were talking in a language he had never heard before.

Casually, so as not to appear uncertain, Marco took a step backward.

His shoes squeaked.

"Hey, Mr. Rent-a-Cop." The gang's leader laughed. "You want to join our party?"

"Do me a favor," said Marco. "Just get the hell out of here."

The leader smiled and scratched his chest. There was paint sprayed across his face. He looked as though he could barely stand.

"You forgot to say 'please,' " he said.

The other kids laughed and began talking in softer voices. Marco had no idea what they were saying, but he guessed they were planning their next move. He considered his options. Running away was definitely one. Saying "please" was not.

Silently, the line of kids began to form a semicircle around him. They were all completely wasted. They were lawless. They were scary. The moment had come, Marco realized. The gang was watching him intently now. He had to act quickly, before someone made a move. Without looking down, Marco reached for his walkie-talkie and raised it to his mouth.

"Proceed as planned," he said, trying to sound as if he was addressing a large number of well-trained and well-armed associates. The plan—as Marco imagined it—was something he was reluctant to do. It was a last resort. He had tried to negotiate, but now he had no alternative, considering the uncooperative nature of the young per-petrators. The plan would be swift and brutal. Some peo-ple might get hurt, but that's just the way it was. When he gave the order to "Proceed as planned," Marco spoke with so much authority he almost believed it himself.

"What the hell are you talking about?" Gavin's loud voice crackled for all to hear.

The color drained from Marco's face as the leader of the gang stepped forward and looked him up and down. For a moment, Marco thought the guy was about to reach in and rip out his heart. Instead, he grabbed the walkie-talkie.

"Hey, Mr. Boss," he said to Gavin. "Why you hiding back there? If you don't want us around, you should come out and tell us yourself, instead of sending a Boy Scout."

The others laughed. There was no answer from Gavin.

The power of positive thinking wasn't working, Marco decided. Maybe he had been a bit hasty, confronting them like this. Being assertive was all well and good, but only in the right situation. Going around asserting yourself sometimes could land you in trouble. Or worse, it could get you killed. Negotiation, Marco decided, was the next step. The trouble was, he had nothing to negotiate with.

There was only one option left.

Marco held out his hand to the gang leader. "Can I have my radio back?"

The leader stared down at Marco's hand, then back up at his face. "Say that again."

Marco tried to hold the leader's gaze. "Can I have my radio back, please?"

The leader smiled.

Marco got the distinct feeling he was about to be hurt. A knife in the guts, maybe. A kick in the balls or a brick over the head. The leader was taking his time to decide.

The gang was getting restless. Something had to happen.

The leader wasn't smiling anymore.

Marco didn't want to die, he decided. Not here. Not like this.

The leader held up the two-way radio in his paint-stained fingers.

"Can you get FM on this?"

Marco shook his head.

The leader was looking at him strangely now, as if he knew him from somewhere.

"Anyone ever tell you you look like Elvis Presley?"

Marco nodded. "Sometimes."

"Not the big fat Elvis. The cool Elvis, before he made all those crappy movies."

"Some of them weren't that bad," said Marco.

"Yeah? Name one."

"*King Creole* was okay."

The leader thought for a moment. "You like Elvis?"

"Sure," said Marco.

"I got his *Best Of*," said the leader. "But it didn't even have 'Blue Suede Shoes.' What kind of *Best Of* is that?"

"You got ripped off," said Marco.

The gang leader shook his head and laughed.

"Here you go, Elvis," he said, handing back the walkie-talkie.

The gang moved away, leaving Marco trembling at the thought of what might have happened. He imagined himself getting beaten to within an inch of his life, while Gavin watched from a safe distance. When he had finally composed himself, Marco turned and walked back to where the night manager was standing.

"Everything under control?" Gavin asked.

"No drama," Marco nodded.

"Stupid kids," said Gavin. "Got nothing better to do. The up side is, none of them are going to live to see twenty, if they keep on like that."

Marco looked at him without speaking.

"Back to work, then," said Gavin.

As the night manager was walking away, Marco called out to him: "You forgot to say 'please.'"

STAFF LOUNGE

Graham, the store manager, had disappeared. No one had seen or heard from him for almost two weeks. According to the rumors that were going around, Graham had nearly died in a parachuting accident. Alternatively, he had been imprisoned for heroin trafficking, kidnapped by political extremists, converted by Seventh Day Adventists, chased by cannibals, fallen into a volcano, killed a pig and drunk its blood, and/or had a sex-change operation and changed his name to Goldie.

Adam was in the staff lounge, washing the cups and plates, when Graham appeared in the doorway. Wearing casual shoes and an open-necked shirt, he came in and made a cup of coffee while Adam wiped down the benches and table.

"How's the old man?" he asked.

"Fine, thanks."

"What's his handicap these days?"

"Bourbon whiskey," said Adam.

Graham laughed.

Louisa walked past the doorway and Graham called her in.

"Do you two know each other?" he asked.

Before Louisa could answer, Adam leaned across and shook her hand.

"It's a pleasure to meet you," he said.

"You too," said Louisa, keeping a straight face.

Graham grinned at them. "I hear you're both doing a terrific job. Apparently there were several comments about you in the box this month, Louisa. Someone even said you were 'inspirational!'"

Adam looked down at his feet.

"Bev said she spoke to you about the full-time position," Graham went on.

"It sounded pretty good," said Louisa. "But I want to continue with nursing."

"Got your exam results back?" asked Graham.

Louisa shook her head. "Not yet."

Graham took a sip of his coffee. "Anyway," he said, "got to fly."

"Are you off on another vacation?" asked Adam.

"What vacation?" Graham laughed. "I'm attending a two-week seminar on management practices."

When Graham was gone, Adam washed his cup and Louisa dried it. Then, together, they organized the coffee mugs according to size and color. They sorted the cutlery, restocked the teabags, and refilled the sugar bowl. It was not often that the lounge received such care and attention.

AISLE 12

"Weevils?"

Abdi had never heard the word before.

"Big fat ones, in the flour," said Jared. "Check it out, homey."

Abdi watched doubtfully as Dylan looked into the paper bag that Jared was holding. The label said *Self-Rising Flour. 2 lb.*

"It's a weevil-fest. They're pigging out!"

"It's weevil-ution, homey. The survival of the fattest."

"It's the eternal struggle."

"It's Good versus Weevil!"

Abdi had no idea what the storeroom boys were talking about. Cautiously, he approached Jared and looked down into the bag.

"See anything?" Dylan asked.

As Abdi looked, Jared puffed up the bag with air, like a bellows, and a cloud of flour flew upward, covering Abdi's face with white dust.

145

Jared and Dylan doubled over, laughing.

"Watch out for that flour, homey!"

"They don't call it *Self-Rising* for nothing."

Before Abdi could speak, he saw Shane, the storeroom manager, standing in the doorway.

"Back to work," he said. "Abdi, can I see you for a moment, please?"

With his face still covered in flour, Abdi followed the storeroom manager into his cramped little office. There was a desk and two chairs, but Shane remained standing. He handed a roll of paper towels to Abdi.

"Here you go," he said. "Wipe that crap off."

Abdi did as he was told.

"What the hell was going on out there?" asked Shane.

"It is not their fault," said Abdi. "It was just a joke."

Shane squinted at Abdi as if he needed sunglasses. "I don't care whose fault it was," he said. "I don't want you clowning around in my store. Understand?"

Abdi nodded. It seemed unfair that he was getting into trouble when the joke had been played on him.

"I did not know . . . ," he started to say, but Shane cut him off.

"I'm not interested," he said, abruptly. "You guys can sort that stuff out for yourselves."

He picked up a leaflet that was lying on his desk. Abdi noticed that his hands and fingers were wrapped in an elastic bandage. "Seen this?" he asked.

Abdi read the title: *Protecting Our Way of Life from a Possible Terrorist Threat.*

He nodded.

"Of course you have," said Shane. "Everyone got one, didn't they? I thought I'd show you anyway, just in case you hadn't."

Shane flipped through the pages until he found what he was looking for.

"If you see anything suspicious in your workplace, it says to call the twenty-four-hour National Security Hot Line. And here," Shane pointed, "it says that all businesses need to review their security measures."

Abdi did not like the look on the storeroom manager's face.

"And what do you think that means?" asked Shane.

Abdi shook his head. "I am not sure."

Shane looked at him for a long time.

"Have you got your papers yet?" he finally asked.

"Not yet."

"How much longer, do you think?"

"The Immigration Department said six more months."

Shane dropped the government leaflet back on his desk.

"Still plenty of time, then."

"I hope so," said Abdi, uncertainly.

"And you're still studying?"

"I am doing English classes and the first year of my hotel management course."

"Still working at the casino?"

"It is part of my training," he said. "I am learning to be a drink waiter."

"Two jobs?" said Shane. "You're a busy boy, aren't you?"

Abdi shifted uncomfortably on his feet.

"Together, they do not make one full-time job," he explained.

Shane looked at his hands and began picking at the threads of the bandage.

"I know about you," he said. "I know about your *circumstances*."

Despite everything he had been through, Abdi felt ashamed.

"I'm not going to insult you," Shane continued, "by asking if you've ever associated with terrorists. Because I know you wouldn't tell me, even if you had. I just want you to know that I'll be here. And I'll be watching you. Understand?"

Abdi made a good waiter. He cleaned up well in a suit. He had a nice smile. He remembered what drinks people ordered: Manhattans, Margaritas, white Russians, and whiskey sours. Abdi knew how to make them, even though he had never tasted one. He was legally old enough, of course, but his religion did not allow alcohol.

He had seen them all in the piano bar: the happy drunks who bumped into walls, the crying drunks who had lost everything in a single hand of poker, the angry drunks who cursed and swore at the security men who escorted them out the door, the pathetic drunks who ate the complimentary pretzel sticks. Abdi would stand behind the bar, mixing their drinks. He would smile at the women and nod at the men. Abdi knew that if he married an American girl, he would automatically get American citizenship. But these were not the kind of girls he could ever marry. They belonged to a different world—a world where he was invisible. There were girls from his country in the apartments where Abdi lived, but he had never spoken to them. In his evening English class, even when the teacher divided the students into pairs, he found it hard to speak to girls. In his country, girls were not allowed to talk to boys alone.

Abdi shared an apartment with three other boys from his country. Each week they pooled their money to buy food and pay the bills. There was never much left over. He worked at the piano bar on Friday and Saturday nights. He was paid from the till and given a staff discount for all his meals and purchases. After work, he would walk home through the city, stopping to look in the bright shop windows, reading the labels and the price tags of things he could never afford. He wondered about the people he saw, what jobs they did and what countries they came from. How many years or generations did it take, he wondered, before a new country felt like home?

* * *

It was the long weekend and the piano bar was full. Abdi was carrying a tray of drinks when a man stood up abruptly and knocked them onto the floor.

"Hey! Watch where the hell you're going!"

"I am sorry," Abdi apologized. "I did not see you."

The man frowned at Abdi.

"Sure is dark in here," he said, as he sat down heavily.

Abdi picked up the spilled drinks and went back to work. He could not be sure if the man had said something racist or not. Had he meant his skin was dark? Abdi looked at the table where the man and his friends were laughing and drinking. His English was not good enough to be absolutely certain. It was a confusing language. Quite often, the way someone said a word could completely change its meaning. It was hard to tell when people were being friendly. He couldn't always tell if they were joking.

Later, as the man was leaving, he came over to shake Abdi's hand.

"No hard feelings," he mumbled, even more drunk than before.

Abdi felt the man put something into his hand. It was a fifty-dollar bill.

"Please. I cannot accept this."

"Try your luck?" The man gave Abdi a wink.

"Pardon me?"

"Go on! You can't win if you don't play."

Abdi had been inside the casino before. He had watched the people sitting patiently by their poker machines. He had seen men stub out the cigarettes they'd only just lit. He had seen women crossing their fingers for luck. Like drinking, gambling was forbidden. But Abdi couldn't help wondering how it would feel to win some money. He wouldn't need to tell anyone.

He took out the fifty-dollar bill and looked at it. It was a lot of money, but not quite enough to buy anything. If he bet it, and won, he might have enough to buy a stereo, a Playstation, or a DVD player. He could tell his friends he had saved up the money. They would all be so happy. No one would ask any questions.

Abdi exchanged his fifty dollars for a single plastic betting chip. It didn't feel like very much money any more. Compared to the amounts that other people were changing, it was nothing. Abdi turned the chip over in his hand. He tried to calculate in his head how many wins it would take, at double or nothing, before he could afford a car or a deposit on a house. He imagined what might happen if he was really lucky. If he won enough money, would the government let him stay?

He thought about leaving his family. The boat trip. The waiting. Wasn't it all just one big gamble?

Cautiously, Abdi approached the roulette table. He watched as the people placed their bets. He knew he could go and get his money back, if he wanted to. With a flick of his wrist, the croupier spun the wheel and rolled the silver ball. Everyone stood at the table and watched until the ball had landed in the square.

"Fifteen red," said the croupier and a woman kissed the crucifix on her necklace.

The man in front of him picked up his betting chips and left the table.

The croupier looked at Abdi. "Are you playing, sir?"

Abdi stepped up to the table and placed his chip on black.

The croupier asked if there were any more bets, then he spun the roulette wheel and rolled the silver ball. And for just one minute while the ball was rolling, before it landed on red and the croupier raked his money away, for that short space of time, Abdi had as much chance as anyone else. His fifty dollars had given him the right to stand there at the table in a suit and bow tie, not as an off-duty waiter, but as one of them, someone whom the croupier had called "sir."

For that one golden moment, it was worth every cent.

Dylan and Jared watched as Abdi took an egg from the package and held it theatrically between his fingers.

"Let me show you something," he said.

Abdi sat cross-legged on the floor and placed the egg in his open hand. With his fingers interlocking, he began to press the egg between his palms. Dylan and Jared could see the effort in his face and the muscles straining in his arms as he pressed harder. But the egg never cracked.

"An egg is a perfect piece of engineering," said Abdi, when he had finished the demonstration. "It is able to withstand the greatest pressure."

"Let me try that, homey."

Jared sat down on the floor and Abdi placed the egg between his palms, making sure it was properly aligned.

"Increase the pressure slowly and steadily," he instructed.

But when Jared tried it, the eggshell immediately broke and the yellow yolk dripped between his fingers, into his lap.

Jared leaped up, wiping the sticky egg off the front of his pants.

"What the hell went wrong?" he snapped.

"I am sorry," Abdi shook his head. "This never happened before."

Dylan tried to calm Jared down.

"No egg-scuses," he told Abdi. "Please egg-splain."

Abdi's face was hard to read.

"I am not sure," he said. "But maybe this egg has weevils?"

"Weevils?"

Dylan raised an eyebrow. Jared looked suspicious. Abdi covered his mouth with his hand. Then, together, they started to laugh.

TRAINING ROOM

Adam found Louisa in the training room, watching a video entitled *So You Want to Work in an Office?* She was sitting up close to the TV screen, and when Adam came into the room she barely glanced at him.

"What are you doing here?" he asked, proceeding to straighten the chairs and pick up the magazines.

When Louisa turned around, her eyes were filled with tears.

"I failed my exam," she said.

AISLE 13

With a bag in each hand and a folding table under one arm, Gina stood outside the shopping center, waiting for the automatic doors to open. Nothing happened. Gina looked up at the movement sensor. There was supposed to be a red light and it was supposed to go green when anyone moved in front of it, but this one had no lights at all. Gina stepped back and put down her things to give her arms a rest. The automatic doors opened and a woman came out. Gina picked up her things, but the doors had closed again before she could squeeze between them. She turned away and moved to the other door. A man was holding it open for his wife, but he let go before Gina got there.

Am I invisible? she wondered.

Gina set up her table at the end of aisle 13, but closer to aisle 14, because thirteen was an unlucky number. Fourteen was a lucky number, she decided, because it was two times seven, and seven was a very lucky number. There were seven days in the week, seven Wonders of the World, seven colors of the rainbow, seven seas, seven dwarves, and seven deadly sins.

Today should be a good day for business, she decided.

Gina laid out seven plastic cups in a neat row, with seven plastic spoons beside them. Seven fitted the length of the table perfectly. Gina plugged in the microwave oven and set up the plastic trays in alphabetical order: fettucine, gnocchi, ravioli, tortellini. She didn't know why she put them in alphabetical order. They just looked better that way. On her blouse, Gina wore a badge that said VISITOR. No one knew what her name was and no one ever asked. Gina didn't work for the supermarket. She worked for an agency. It was her job to promote food by asking people to sample it. Today, it was pasta.

"Roma's Pasta. *La Prima del Mondo*. Would you like to try some, ma'am?"

"Good morning, sir! Have you tried our fettucine?"

"How are you today, ma'am? Would you like some tortellini?"

Gina had done in-store promotions for party pies, cocktail franks, curry puffs, cheese and crackers, frozen yogurt, gelato, sorbet, canned soup, veggie burgers, mini–dim sums, and flavored milk. She was good at her job. It wasn't just that she knew all about the products, or that she was neat and tidy. It wasn't even because she had a friendly face and happy smile. Gina was good at her job because she cared about people and what they thought of the product. It was important to her that the customer was satisfied. It felt good to hear the customer say they liked the product and were interested in buying it.

"The ravioli is excellent, ma'am! Only the finest ingredients."

"It's a traditional recipe, sir. It has no preservatives. No artificial color or flavor."

"Have you tried the gnocchi, ma'am? It's 97 percent fat-free."

During her lunch break, Gina went to the food court. There was an Italian takeout, but she had seen enough pasta for one day, so she bought a sandwich instead. She asked for a salad sandwich without cheese, but they gave her cheese anyway.

Gina found a table to sit at. Over by the ATMs there was a statue of an old man in a purple cloak and a tall pointy hat. *Ask the Wise Wizard* said the sign above his head. When Gina had finished her sandwich, she went over and put a coin into the Wise Wizard's slot. The Wise Wizard made a whizzing noise, followed by an electronic beep. Then a slip of paper popped out of his hand.

It said: *Today is the tomorrow you thought about yesterday.*

Gina wasn't certain. Was the Wise Wizard only fooling or was it a riddle she had to solve? If today was the tomorrow she had thought about yesterday, then tomorrow, today would be yesterday. But if today was tomorrow yesterday and would be yesterday tomorrow, if yesterday had once been tomorrow and tomorrow would soon be yesterday, then yesterday could become tomorrow without ever being today, as far as Gina could see. And if today had disappeared, then so had yesterday and tomorrow.

Which left what?

As Gina looked up from her slip of paper, the automatic doors opened. But there was no one there. They had opened by themselves. At that moment it seemed to Gina that a strange light had entered the food court. The noise intensified and the air felt electric. It was something undefinable. A kind of energy, she decided. A *presence*.

Something happened to Gina. For a moment everything seemed new and unfamiliar—not only the place she was standing in, but also the things she was thinking, even the feeling of who she was. High on the roof of the food court she saw a sparrow perched on one of the rafters. A bird inside the house is considered bad luck by some people, but for Gina it was a sign of something else. The bird was a symbol for freedom. There was no today, no yesterday, and no tomorrow. There was only now, and she was there to see it.

* * *

After her lunchbreak, Gina returned to her table at the end of aisle 13. She plugged in the microwave oven and set up the trays of pasta, from fettucine to tortellini. She laid out the plastic cups with their little plastic spoons lined up like soldiers. They looked like a little army, standing at attention, keeping their eyes straight ahead and their faces blank, without expression.

"Roma's Pasta. Would you like to try some, ma'am? It's 97 percent fat-free."

But the first customer shook her head.

"How can something be 97 percent fat-free?" she asked.

Gina smiled and tried to explain, but the woman didn't believe her. When she was gone, Gina shifted the plastic cups slightly to make them more evenly spaced. She noticed the cups and spoons were made by different companies. The cups were more transparent than the spoons. But the spoons had to be stronger, so they wouldn't bend. Plastic was an amazing invention. You could make just about anything out of it.

"Good afternoon, sir. Would you like some ravioli?"

The customer frowned at the label on the package.

"All natural ingredients?" he scoffed. "That's false advertising, isn't it?"

Gina smiled and reassured him, but the man had made up his mind. When he had moved on, she stepped out from behind her table to greet the next customer.

"Excuse me, ma'am. Would you be interested in—"

"No, thank you." The woman kept on walking.

"Roma's Pasta, sir?"

"Who the hell is Roma?"

Gina glanced at her watch and straightened her skirt. If the next customer was a man, Gina decided, she would ask about his busy lifestyle. If it was a woman, she would ask about her children.

"Good afternoon—"

"What's so good about it?"

Gina reheated the pasta and tried rearranging the plastic cups in other ways. Instead of laying them out in a straight line, she experimented with triangles and circles. She put the spoons inside the cups, to make it easier for customers to take them. It made no difference. None of the supermarket shoppers was interested in Gina. They hurried past her table, barely giving her a sideways glance. When she greeted them, they mumbled something and kept on walking. When she asked them questions, they shook their heads and looked away. People made a detour just to avoid her. Others made up lame excuses. They had already eaten. They were vegetarian or they were trying to lose weight. Gina didn't believe them. She knew they were lying. It was almost as if everyone in the store was deliberately avoiding her. It felt like a conspiracy, as though someone somewhere must be telling them to stay away from her. Gina watched each customer as they approached. Her smile felt painful, as if it were stuck to her face. She had stopped speaking to them now. What was the point of speaking to them, when they were all so rude to her? What was the point of her even being there?

She glanced at her watch again. It had hardly moved since the last time she looked. What would she say to her boss? Would she lie or tell the truth? She felt a hollow feeling deep inside. It started in her stomach and expanded into her chest. It spread across her shoulders and up her neck. There was nothing she could do to control it. Her jaw muscles locked as she opened her mouth wide to let the feeling out. It rose like a shadow from the depths of her soul, and once it had started it felt as though it would never stop. Gina covered her mouth with her hand as she yawned an almighty yawn.

Finally, the time came. Gina took off her visitor's badge and began to pack up her display. One by one, she scooped out the pasta from the little plastic cups and threw it into the garbage can. She had already reheated it several times over. She was half packed up when she heard the sound of wheels approaching. A cart appeared, with two boys riding on top. They rounded the corner at full speed, almost colliding with her.

"Any food left?" asked one.

"We're starving," said the other.

There were two servings of tortellini remaining, so Gina

popped them into the microwave for thirty seconds. She looked at their name tags.

"It's simple to prepare," she said wearily. "Just heat and serve."

"Sounds good in theory," said the one called Dylan.

"Trouble is," said the one called Jared, "the only instruction we understand is *eat.*"

Gina watched them as they wolfed down the tortellini. "What do you think?"

"Excellent taste!" mumbled Dylan.

His friend agreed.

"If I was on death row, homey, I might just choose the tortellini for my last meal."

"It might not be on the menu."

"If you specifically asked for tortellini, homey, I'm sure they could call out and get some delivered."

The one called Dylan considered it. "I'd have a burger, I think."

The one called Jared grinned. "You want to be fried with that?"

Gina tried to smile.

"It's all-natural ingredients," she murmured. "And 97 percent fat-free."

It was all she could think of to say.

Gina walked out of the supermarket with her bags in her hands and her table under one arm. The Wise Wizard seemed to smile at her as she crossed the food court. It was not a nasty smile, exactly, but not a nice one, either.

Today is the tomorrow you thought about yesterday.

And tomorrow, Gina knew, she would be doing the same job in another supermarket.

The automatic doors were still open, and two men in orange reflector jackets were busy trying to fix them. Gina thought they looked suspiciously like *X-File* types, involved in some kind of cover-up. Instead of there being a presence in the room, she felt an emptiness—like a swimming pool without water—as if something had drained away. What did it matter about yesterday, today, and tomorrow? Everything looked as if it was made of cardboard. She felt as though she could reach out and poke her hand through it. She looked up at the ceiling, searching for the little bird, but it had flown away, of course.

Gina walked to the door. Then, at the last minute, she turned and walked back to the Wise Wizard. She found another coin and put it in the slot. But before she let it go, she took it out again. No. Instead of asking the Wise Wizard she would toss the coin and decide for herself. Heads, she would quit her stupid job. Tails, she wouldn't.

With a flick of her thumb, Gina tossed the coin high into the air. But when she went to catch it, she missed and it slipped through her fingers. The coin fell to the floor and began to roll slowly away.

Gina let it go. She had already made up her mind.

STOREROOM

Adam had done his utmost. He had tried being cheerful, resourceful, helpful, enthusiastic, diligent, attentive, considerate, conscientious, assiduous, courteous, meticulous, flexible, receptive, dependable, industrious, and responsible, but as far as he knew, Louisa hadn't noticed any of it. Being the perfect worker made the time pass more quickly, but it wasn't going to get him the girl. After several days of effort, Adam was exhausted. He practiced saying "Not a problem, not a problem," over and over when no one else was around, but the more he said it, the less convincing he sounded. His face hurt from smiling too much. Now he knew what the checkout chicks complained of. He was fed up with being Mr. Nice Guy.

On his break Adam borrowed Jared's cell phone to call the TV repairman to see if his set was fixed yet.

"What do you mean, you haven't even looked at it?"

"I didn't know it was important," the TV repairman told him.

"Not important?" he exploded. "It's my television!"

Adam gave the guy an earful and hung up. In a fury, he filled Goliath the box crusher single-handedly, then wrestled so violently with the block of crushed cardboard that Jared and Dylan heard and came running to applaud him. They had never seen anyone so fired up. Adam was mad as hell and he wasn't going to take it anymore.

CUSTOMER SERVICE

The man at the Customer Service counter was shouting into his cell phone as he handed Louisa a crumpled-up note. He was in his thirties, had broad shoulders, and was wearing a waterproof jacket with sponsors' names written across it.

"Give me a hand, will ya? I can't read a word of this."

Louisa uncrumpled the shopping list. The illegible squiggles could have said anything from apples to zebras.

"She's gone out with her friends," said the man, resuming his phone conversation. "I have to cook for myself again, the second time this month!"

Louisa tried to hand back the note but he ignored her.

"That's it, man. They don't appreciate us . . . Hang on, buddy."

"It's impossible," Louisa told him. "I can't make out a single word."

The man gave Louisa a dirty look. He screwed up

the shopping list and threw it away. "I give up, man. Useless stupid checkout chick. She probably can't read anyway."

"Pick that up, please," Louisa asked, but the man ignored her.

Unaccountably, her eyes filled with tears. She was exhausted. She had failed her anatomy exam and now she had this pig to deal with. It was too much.

When Louisa lifted her head, she saw Adam coming toward her on a shopping cart pushed by Jared and Dylan. He was holding a mop in his hand like a knight in shining armor, riding to her rescue.

Adam jumped off the cart to confront the man in the racing jacket. His face was red and he looked furious.

"You heard her," he pointed at the crumpled paper on the floor. "She asked you to pick that up."

The man in the racing jacket glanced at Jared and Dylan who were standing on either side of Adam. He put his phone away, picked up his shopping list, and walked out of the store.

When he was gone, Louisa looked at Adam.

"My hero!" she laughed. Then she broke off a daisy and gave it to him.

AISLE 14

Cameron, the produce manager, opened his Lonely Planet travel guide and ran his finger down the list of countries. Fiji was out of the question—too far and expensive. Costa Rica was cool, but all his friends had been to Costa Rica. Morocco was risky; lots of terrorists were still out there in the desert somewhere. The Middle East was out—more terrorists. Africa? Too many unexploded land mines. The Philippines? Too sleazy. The Amazon? What the hell was there to do in the Amazon?

Myanmar?

Cameron turned to the page and started to read. Myanmar was the new name for Burma. It was a Buddhist country run by a military dictatorship. There were no terrorists but the visas were tight and there were areas where tourists were prohibited. Cameron was planning his honeymoon. He wanted it to be special. (Adventurous, to impress the girl, but not dangerous.) Myanmar, the book said, was a beautiful country. It was cheap. The fruit was good, and there were some great beaches. Going there and spending money would be good for the economy but would also be interpreted as support for the military dictatorship. It was a decision each individual tourist had to make for themselves.

Myanmar sounded cool, Cameron had to admit.

Nicola, the dairy manager, walked into the room and Cameron immediately covered his travel book with a sheet of paper. "Dill . . . parsley . . . basil . . . coriander," he murmured to himself, ticking a few boxes. "Morning, Nicola!"

"What are you doing?"

"Local orders."

"You know what I mean."

There was a game Cameron liked to play in his head. All the girls he'd ever been out with were like pieces of fruit. Some were peaches, some were mangoes, some were figs, and some were lemons. Nicola, he decided, was a pineapple.

"Do I?" he grinned.

"That's Amanda's desk," said Nicola.

"*Was* Amanda's desk."

"And will be again, when Graham comes back."

"*If* Graham comes back."

"What do you mean, *if*?"

"Haven't you heard the rumors?"

"All I've heard," said Nicola, "is that Graham is on leave. Did Amanda say you could use her desk while she's the acting manager?"

"I thought it was cool. You know, first come, first served."

"It doesn't work that way, Cameron."

"Which way does it work, Nicola?"

"You've already moved your stuff! What time did you get here this morning?"

"I had a delivery."

"And how long have you been sitting there, guarding that stupid desk?"

"I have been working, Nicola. Doing produce isn't like doing dairy. There actually is some work involved."

"You're pathetic."

"Do you want this desk?"

"Not if I have to fight you for it."

"Well, that's settled, then."

Scott, the trainee manager, walked into the room. "Morning, team!"

"Cameron has taken Amanda's desk," said Nicola. "He says she may not be coming back."

Scott looked at Cameron. "What's the story, bud?"

Cameron shrugged. If women were like fruit, then men must be vegetables. Scott, he decided, was a cabbage.

"I needed more space," he said. "That's cool, isn't it?"

"It's not cool," said Nicola. "Not with me, anyway."

"Did Amanda say you could have it?" asked Scott.

"She cleaned it out, didn't she?"

"Graham's in the hospital," he said. "That's what I heard. Heart attack, probably."

"I meant about the desk," said Scott.

Nicola shook her head. "I've been in this office longer than you have, Cameron."

"I'm doing Amanda's job, while she's doing Graham's," said Scott.

"And I'm doing Scott's job while he's doing Amanda's," said Nicola.

"And I'm getting married next month," said Cameron. "But you don't hear *me* complaining."

"That's pathetic!" said Nicola.

"Come on, bud," said Scott. "Be reasonable."

Cameron turned his back on them. "Some of us have work to do," he said.

"You won't get away with this," said Nicola.

"Damage, freshness, quantity, size . . ." Cameron pretended he wasn't listening any more.

Nicola put her hands on her hips. "You can't guard it all day. The minute you leave this room, that's it, buddy. No more desk!"

Cameron swiveled around to face her.

"I have to go down to the freezer now," he said. "I assume I will get back to find everything just as I've left it."

"You can assume whatever you want," said Nicola.

"I have some very important documents here. I'd appreciate it if you didn't touch anything."

Cameron stood up. Nicola stepped to one side to let him leave, but then he saw the look on her face.

"You wouldn't dare, Nicola!"

"Oh, wouldn't I, Cameron?"

"Come on, guys," said Scott. "This is getting stupid."

Cameron moved toward the doorway. Nicola moved toward the desk. It was a standoff.

"I'm warning you, Nicola!"

"Are you threatening me, Cameron?"

Cameron turned abruptly and walked out the door. As soon as he was gone, Nicola went to the desk and swept all his papers onto the floor. Within seconds, Cameron had returned. As he came back into the room—face red and fists clenched—Nicola spotted the guidebook.

"What's this?"

"None of your business," Cameron fumed.

He tried to grab it, but she wouldn't let go. There was a brief scuffle and the sound of ripping paper as a picture of a golden Buddha floated gently to the floor.

Then, from inside the store, there was a sudden loud explosion.

A middle-aged customer placed her shopping basket on Chloe's counter.

"I won't be a moment," she said. "I've forgotten grapes."

The customer behind her looked at Chloe. "Is she allowed to do that?"

Chloe shrugged.

The second woman looked around, but there was no sign of the first.

"I'm in a bit of a hurry," she told Chloe. "I'm sure she won't mind."

The second woman put her basket to the front, but before Chloe could begin scanning, the first woman returned.

"Do you mind?" she said, trying to push past the second woman.

"Yes. I do mind, actually."

"But I was here first."

"You went away."

"And then I came back."

They both turned and looked at Chloe.

"I told you I would only be a moment," said the first woman.

"We didn't think you were coming back," said the second.

"Well, you were wrong, weren't you?"

"It says eight items or less. How many do you have?"

"I don't know. I haven't counted."

"I'd say you've got at least ten."

"In other supermarkets, for your information, they allow twelve."

"Not in this supermarket, though. Can't you read the sign?"

"That's rather petty, don't you think?"

"You're the one who's being petty."

They both looked at Chloe again, but Chloe wasn't taking sides.

"This is outrageous!" said the first woman.

"Who do you think you are?" said the second.

"I'm going to speak to the manager."

"I'm going to write a letter."

The first woman tried to place her basket in front of the other's, but the second woman stopped her. They struggled briefly with the basket. In the scuffle, the bag of grapes fell to the floor and the second woman began crushing them with her heels. The first woman took the other's basket and tipped out all the items. The second woman was about to retaliate when, from inside the store, there was a sudden loud explosion.

Adam was kneeling down, stocking the lowest shelf when it happened. There was a sudden loud explosion, then he fell to the floor and lay there, stunned. When Adam opened his eyes, people were standing over him. His hands and clothes were covered in blood. There was blood on the floor and broken glass everywhere.

"Oh my God!"

"What the hell happened?"

"He's been shot!"

More people arrived. Customers and staff gathered around him. Judging from their shocked expressions, Adam thought he must be badly hurt. There certainly was a lot of blood.

"Get a doctor!"

"Call an ambulance!"

"Try not to move!"

"Don't worry, Andy. You're going to be okay."

"Try not to speak."

Adam felt faint. "Louisa?" he murmured.

"Quick! Someone get Louisa! She's a nurse!"

Louisa arrived and knelt down beside him. She took out her handkerchief and gently began wiping the blood from his face. When he looked up and saw her, Adam knew everything would be OK. Louisa would save him.

"I can't feel a thing," he said.

"You're going to be fine," she assured him.

"What I mean is, I'm not hurt."

"It's just tomato sauce," said Louisa. "One of the bottles exploded."

There was no sickroom, so they took Adam to the manager's office and sat him in Graham's chair. Amanda found him a clean shirt, then she went to see Bev about a form he would need to sign before he could be sent home. Adam was dazed. He was safe, uninjured, and now he and Louisa finally had a reason to be alone together. He thought about asking her to reexamine him for broken bones.

Louisa shut the office door. Adam took a deep breath. Now was the perfect moment.

"How are you feeling?" she asked.

"Lucky," he said.

Louisa took Adam's wrist and felt his pulse.

"You're very flushed," she said. "You're probably still in shock."

Adam felt Louisa's soft cool fingers against his skin. He remembered the daisy she had given him. He had taken it home and put it in water, and as the petals began to wither he had counted them, one by one. *She loves me . . . She loves me not . . .* At the end, it was hard to be certain. There was a gap with one petal missing.

Louisa let go of his wrist.

Adam hesitated. He was letting the perfect moment get away. Adam watched the perfect moment pack its bags. He followed it as it walked out the door and climbed into the backseat of a very fast car. He stood there as the perfect moment wound up its window and waved good-bye. He did nothing as it sped off into the distance. Adam let it go. The perfect moment was miles away now, and it wasn't coming back.

"You'll make a good nurse," he said instead.

"If I ever finish my course," Louisa sighed.

"You only failed one subject."

"They want me to repeat the whole year."

"That's not fair."

Louisa shrugged. "I got moved up a grade at school, so I'm really too young to be in college, anyway."

Adam sat up. "You got moved ahead? You're . . . still seventeen? We're the *same age*?"

Louisa nodded. "Our birthdays are in the same month."

Adam tried to stop himself grinning. "How do you know when my birthday is?"

"I've been helping Bev with the pay slips. I hope you don't think I was nosy. Actually, I'm three days younger than you."

"You're three days *younger* than me?"

By the time Amanda returned, Adam was completely recovered. He wanted to go back to work, he said, but Amanda insisted he take the rest of the day off. He signed the form Amanda gave him. She offered to drive him home in her car, but he said he would be fine. Outside, in the parking lot, he collected the shopping carts, then he helped an elderly lady onto the bus.

When Adam got home, there was a message on the answering machine to say that his TV had been fixed and was ready to be picked up. Instead of phoning them back, Adam went out into the garden. The trees were singing, the flowers were humming, and there were countless petals all over the grass.

AISLE 15

It was a hot day. The air-conditioning was working overtime. Amanda, the acting store manager, stood by the sink with the envelope in her hand. Beside her stood Cameron, the acting grocery manager; Scott, the acting produce manager; and Nicola, the acting trainee manager. The workers were seated in front of them or standing with their backs to the wall. The staff lounge was so crowded, there was no room to move.

"It gives me great pleasure to announce our new Employee of the Month."

Amanda reassured the workers that as far as she was concerned, they were all Employees of the Month. The most important thing in any work-place, she said, was teamwork. With teamwork, there was nothing that couldn't be achieved. Without it, their achievements would be limited. Amanda was excited about the future, she said. She was proud of the company she worked for and proud of the people she worked with. She had great dreams, she said, of a better, more productive workplace.

Amanda spoke in a clear, confident voice. She established eye contact with all the people in the room. Her hands reached out to convey the importance of what she was saying, but the words she chose were dull and repetitive. Future achievements. Productive teamwork. Future teamwork. Productive achievements. Teamwork achievements. Productive futures. Amanda's words were like a box of wet matches, a lighter without fluid, a bulb without a filament. The workers had heard them all, too many times before. It didn't take long for each of them to drift away and become lost in their own thoughts.

Dylan worried that there weren't any windows. He wondered how long the oxygen would last with so many people crammed into such a small space. Rahel thought about how many of her cousins she would need to invite to her wedding and if she would remember their names. Abdi wondered which country Rahel was from and what language she spoke. Chloe tried to imagine if Scott and Cameron had ever compared their dates with her and in how much detail. Wyn recalled the appropriate number range in the Dewey Decimal System: 300–399—Social Sciences. Jared counted the minutes on his watch, to calculate how much he was getting paid to do nothing. Emma imagined the Academy Awards, the nominees' brave faces and the smile of the winner. Louisa wondered if there was enough available staff for the registers. And Adam noticed how her face looked even more beautiful since he had found out she was three days younger than he was.

When Amanda had said all there was to say about productivity in the workplace, health and safety issues, career opportunities, having the right attitude, and the people who worked in a supermarket being like "one big happy family," she tore open the envelope and took out a piece of paper.

"Some people dream of worthy accomplishments," she said, "others stay awake and do them. And there is no other worker I can think of who is more deserving of this month's award. It gives me great pleasure, therefore, to announce that the Employee of the Month is . . . Andy! I mean . . . Adam!"

Amanda pinned the badge to Adam's shirt. She gave him his movie tickets and his plaque with the picture of someone standing on top of a mountain. Scott, the acting produce manager, took a Polaroid photograph and everyone clapped because they had to.

"Congratulations!" said Amanda, shaking Adam's hand.

"There's something I want to say," he told her.

Amanda looked at him oddly. No one had ever made an acceptance speech before.

This was Adam's big chance. In his mind, it was the perfect opportunity to declare publicly how he felt about

Louisa. After all, Louisa was his inspiration. She was the reason he had been named Employee of the Month.

He cleared his throat and took a deep breath.

"I would just like to say," he cleared his throat again. "On my first day in this job, I was in trouble," he glanced at Amanda. "I thought, *This is stupid. What am I doing here?* And it is stupid, I know." Adam looked at the now-familiar faces of his coworkers. "But then I started meeting people and I realized . . ." He glanced at Louisa, who had tears in her eyes. "I realized I could learn things. I thought I knew it all, but I was wrong."

Amanda tried to cut him off. "Thank you, Adam, for those . . . words."

Then, to Adam's great surprise, everyone cheered.

Adam was in aisle 15, restocking the shelves with Doggy Treats, when Louisa came up to him.

"Need a hand?"

Adam knew the box was almost empty. The job was almost done.

"That would be great, thanks."

Louisa placed the last package of Doggy Treats on the shelf, then stepped back to look at it. "It seems a bit messy, don't you think?"

"It does a bit."

"Do you think we should start again?"

"If you'd like to."

Together, they took down the Doggy Treats and put them back in the box.

"I hope I'm not being bossy," she said.

"Not at all."

Adam watched Louisa restock the shelves in a different way, shuffling packages of Doggy Treats as if they were playing cards.

"How did you learn to do that?" he asked.

"It's just experience."

"Are you really going to work here full-time?"

"Of course not."

"But I thought . . ."

"My mom called up the Faculty of Nursing and made an appointment to see my counselor. I have never seen her so angry. In the end, the counselor agreed to let me take a makeup exam, which means I won't have to repeat. If I pass, of course."

"Price check on register six . . ." came an announcement. *"Price check on register six . . ."*

They both ignored it.

"Why do you stare at me sometimes?" asked Louisa.

"I don't stare at you, do I?"

"Yes, you do. You stare at me as if I'm doing something wrong."

"You never do anything wrong. If I watch you some-times, it's because I admire you."

"You admire me?"

"Professionally," Adam explained. "As the Employee of the Month."

"*Could I* please *have a staff member to register six to do a price check!*"

"So now *I'm* allowed to stare at *you*," said Louisa.

Adam smiled. "It's pretty silly, isn't it?"

"The movie tickets are good."

"Yeah. The movie tickets are good."

"I haven't used mine yet," said Louisa. "I've been too busy."

"What will you go and see?"

"I don't even know what's playing. Do you?"

Adam took a deep breath. "We could . . ."

"*There's a customer waiting, so could someone please come to register six right now, if it's not too much trouble. Thank you!*"

"I should go and see what they want," said Louisa.

"No, you shouldn't."

"It sounds important."

"More important than this?" said Adam, holding up a package of Doggy Treats.

Louisa smiled. "Do you think I work too hard?"

"You could have more fun," said Adam.

"More fun?" Louisa stopped smiling.

He could have kicked himself. "I didn't mean . . ."

They finished restocking the shelves together, then she turned to him.

"Have you taken any more photos?"

Adam shook his head.

"What about that one of you, beside the river. You said you would get me a copy, remember?"

"But you said . . . I didn't know . . . I threw it away."

"But it was such a good photo!"

"It was?"

"You looked so deep and meaningful."

"I did?"

"And not at all like a complete idiot."

"You're teasing me, aren't you?"

Louisa grinned. "You said I should have more fun."

When Adam looked at her, he knew the perfect moment had returned. A bus had just pulled up and the perfect moment had hopped off it, looking scruffy and reckless.

"There's something I've been meaning to ask you," he said.

Louisa smiled.

"What are you doing after work?" she said.